The Dictionary of Someone Else's Child

Jay Ganguly

ISBN: 9798655851368

DEDICATION

For my Baba

The best and wisest man I have ever known!

If half (or even a quarter of) the people on this earth were as good as you, we'd be living in paradise.

Happy Father's Day!

ACKNOWLEDGMENTS

A big thank you to all the good folks who have read (or been forcefully subjected to) any of my writings and encouraged me to write more. I might fancy myself to be a writer, but it wouldn't make me one unless someone actually reads it, yes?

1 PREFACE

Dictionary (*noun*):
A collection of words explaining their meaning and usage, usually arranged in alphabetical order. May be for a language in general or specific to a particular field/topic.
Examples: (1) Oxford English Dictionary, (2) Black's Law Dictionary

Someone Else's Child (*noun, figure of speech*):
Some random overachieving kid that parents/guardians/teachers use as an example or comparison when trying to get the kids to behave or learn something. Especially prevalent in Asian cultures.
Examples: (1) Look at A's daughter, she studies for six hours every day after school, that's why she ranks first. (2) Z's son is so polite and caring, did you see how much he respects his elders?

***

Hello, there. This is Seccy. What's with the weird name and introduction, you say? Well, I'm just explaining the title of the book. My book. Ah, it feels good to say that. But is it really a book? Well, dictionaries are also books, and the explanations in this dictionary are very specific to a certain topic – "Someone Else's Child".

I, too, am one of the samples of the quintessential (and much dreaded) "Someone Else's Child" – literally as well as figuratively. "SEC" is the abbreviation for that, which I will be using throughout the text, when referring to the general concept of SEC rather than a specific person.

Most people call me Seccy, and that is what I will be called throughout the text. Oh, and the "cc" is pronounced as "k" as in "Chewbacca" or "Rebecca" and not as an "x" like in "sexy". Although, that'd be really cool.

I'd quite like that.

Also, I'm the second child in my family, so "Seccy" actually has its origins in that (rather than "SEC" – I mean, it'd be weird if your own parents called you "Someone Else's Child" even if you're adopted).

So, anyway, I've put together a collection of words (yup, that's a dictionary) that I relate to (or other people relate to me). Why, you ask? Because I felt like it.

I'm an author now. What's one more thing for your peer group to envy?

2 ACHIEVEMENT

Achievement (*noun*):

Winning, gaining success or recognition, getting something with effort or skill.

Examples: (1) She won the first prize! (2) He finally managed to iron his shirt without burning it!

***

Achievement, naturally, is one of the most basic characteristics of a "SEC".

Unless you achieve something (or a lot of things), how would you be worthy of being used an example for other kids? In fact, the more stellar your achievements, the better!

Getting top grades, winning prizes – those are basic things. Exemplary conduct is another. Achievements can be skill-based or effort-based, both kinds are acceptable.

As for me, I'm a mix of both. Well, I was adopted in the first place because of my IQ, you know? Well, partly, at least. I'm not complaining – I've had a wonderful life since Mum and Dad picked me up from the orphanage about twenty years ago. I was five, and I had an IQ of 165. Yes, I was tested.

You see, Mum and Dad are super-smart people, and they needed smart kids – it wasn't out of malice or anything, but it's just that they didn't think they could raise a kid that wasn't approximately as smart as them (oh, boy – I said this to them once – well, I was in my teenage rebellion phase and dealing with existential angst – and they got so mad that they grounded me for a week). Now we joke about it and tease them that instead of leaving it to chance and taking a risk with the natural process and begetting dumb kids, they went and adopted three high-IQ kids (although it wasn't on purpose – it just sort of happened) – which is not quite untrue. I'm the middle one.

My older brother is your textbook genius. Beyond genius, actually. His IQ is well over 200 and he's got an eidetic memory. His brain is…it is beyond comprehension, really. He can think of things no one can. He's hardly ever wrong. He is amazing. Sometimes, I wonder if he was artificially manufactured – he's that awesome. My Big Brother is the stuff of legends. I adore him, and I'm also very, very proud of him. I won't be surprised at all if he wins the Nobel prize before his thirty fifth birthday (he turns thirty this year). The prizes he has already won fill up an entire hall in our home.

Overachieving as he is, though, he is also socially inept. In terms of brain-skills, no one can beat Big Brother – well, to the best of my knowledge. He is the smartest person I know (and let me tell you, I know some *really* smart people all over the world, including laureates of prestigious as well as obscure awards – thanks to Mum and Dad, who are also pretty amazing themselves). So, while Big Brother is the perfect skill-based achiever when it comes to brains, he's deplorable in terms of life-skills. It is a little funny (and adorable) that Big Brother, who can argue at par with renowned mathematicians, scientists, philosophers (basically any learned person) thrice his age, flounders when asked, "How are you doing?" Mind you, he will have a very detailed response to, "*What* are you doing?" Similarly, he can do all sorts of complicated calculations for a rocket propulsion (and that's not even his field of work), but he still manages to burn his toast on a daily basis. In a *toaster.* He's rather cute that way, though I worry for his future spouse. We all do. If he ever chooses to marry, that is. It's not that his EQ is low – in fact, he's probably the most empathetic among the three of us. It's just that he doesn't know what to do with it. He's the first to know what someone is feeling, but more often than not, he has no clue how to respond…or feels too shy to respond. Mum says it's because all his senses are enhanced and he gets overwhelmed easily. Dad says it's because they focussed on his education too much and forgot to teach him everyday things. Someone he dated in college told him (while breaking up with him) that he was too pampered and sheltered to be a "real" person (along with a lot of other malicious stuff) – oh, boy, that was a disaster. Big Brother was heartbroken, and it took us days to coax him out. Of course, Little Sister and I extracted appropriate revenge (and an apology to Big Brother) from the other party. We're a close-knit family, you know? We watch out for each other…and we do tend to be a bit overprotective.

As for my younger sister, she's another genius – well, naturally, all three of us were adopted because we are extraordinary (oh, I can totally imagine the furious look Mum will give me for saying this). Little Sister's IQ is much higher than mine (but not as high as Big Brother's), and she's the most gregarious among us. She's also the coolest, the fittest and the most talented. You give her a musical instrument and she'll play it within five minutes even if she's never seen it before. You give her a weapon and she'll wield it perfectly. You give her a vehicle and she'll run it like she's been doing it all her life. She's only twenty, but she can beat anyone in a fight. If she'd been born a few centuries ago, she'd have been the empress that unified the world. I'm not joking – she really would have. She can not only fight, she's also a master strategist. And on top of that, she's so beautiful that Big Brother and I have been fending off unsavoury suitors for *ages*. Not that she needs us to, she can beat anyone into a pulp, including us. But we want to spare her the irritation, you know? She's dating someone now – and she absolutely refuses to tell me who it is. Well, Big Brother knows and he's keeping an eye on the matter, so it's ok for now. If this person harms a single hair on her pretty little head, though…

As for me – I'm fairly average compared to my siblings, but I'd be considered quite an achiever myself when I step out of the house. I've always had top grades (that's a given in our family – although, there was this one time that I came second in my class, and I was so ashamed – and scared that Mum and Dad would send me back to the orphanage – that I ran away from home. It took Mum and Dad almost two days to find me. I got the scolding of a lifetime, but it was also the first time I learnt that I was loved, and that I had a family which would not abandon me even if I wasn't perfect. Fortunately, it was before Little Sister was adopted, or I'd have been beaten into a pulp by her. Or maybe not. In any case, I'd rather not find out!). I'm good with extra-curricular activities (good enough to be one of the best among my peers, but nothing compared to my Little Sister, of course) – I can sing, dance and paint, and I'm moderately ok at sports. Nowhere close to pro-levels, but I used to win a few medals whenever I entered competitions. Within the family, I'm the most normal person – and Mum often says I'm the only one with any common sense. I also head a highly profitable company. Technically, it is a subsidiary of the family's flagship company that I was given to handle when I graduated, but the behind-the-scenes fact is that Mum and Dad formed a new company and gave it to me to play with on my fifteenth birthday. I've been running it right from the start. Not too many people know about it, but it's not exactly a secret.

Now, I'm sure you're wondering why this relatively average Seccy is the SEC instead of my extraordinary Big Brother and Little Sister, right? Certainly, their achievements are far above mine. And that's exactly where the problem is. They're outliers, both of them. You could scour the earth, but you won't find two people as magnificent as my siblings. They are god-like creatures of legend. They will be recorded in history. Books will be written about them. They'll have museums, awards, roads and things named after them. They are incomparable.

SEC, on the other hand, is an average human construct, necessarily comparable. Yes, achievements are mandatory for a SEC, but achievability is also important. Can Big Brother's accomplishments be duplicated with acquired skills and efforts? No chance. What about Little Sister's? Nope. But my success? Oh yes. It might take someone with lower IQ a little more time and effort than it's taken me, but it can be done, if similar resources are provided. In fact, one of my long-term business plans includes an incubator company to promote exactly that.

You see, the whole point of a SEC is his/her use as an achievable reference point to encourage the target to achieve similar success. The reference point should not be too intimidating or out of reach; the target needs to be able to see that with some skills (either innate or acquired) and effort, he/she can achieve the desired goal. A SEC has to be comparable.

I'll give you an example. Big Brother and I once participated in an essay competition at school – him in the senior section and me in the junior section. We both won first prizes in our sections. However, Big Brother's essay was so good that the judges declared that he was beyond ranking and sent his essay to be published in a peer-reviewed journal of an Ivy-League University (it did get published). Would the kids who won the second and third places ever be able to compare to that? On the other hand, I won the first prize with a margin of 3 points. The girl who got the second place could easily topple me in the next competition, right? That's what you call comparable   and   achievable.

3 BRILLIANT

Brilliant (*adjective*):

Clever or talented – well, basically a person who shines brighter than his/her peers in terms of intellect or talent.

Example: That ten-year-old plays the violin like a professional, isn't she just brilliant?

***

This is self-explanatory, really. How would you be compared to someone by your people if that person didn't outshine you? Again, in the SEC context, the outshining difference must be believable and reachable.

I'll explain with proper anecdotes. So, like I said before, my Big Brother is the smartest person ever, and my Little Sister is the most talented person ever. Are they brilliant? Yes, absolutely. They shine brighter than everyone else. In fact, they're so brilliant that they leave everyone bedazzled. But they are not SEC, because they are not comparable.

Like the time when I was adopted. I was five. I didn't have a particularly bad time at the orphanage from what I can remember, but I do remember being hungry and bored all the time. Once I was beaten up by the resident bullies because I scored well on a test and the teacher praised me in class, and especially told the bullies that they should be a good boy like me. (That was probably my first experience of being used as a SEC.) Naturally, the bullies were not pleased. They cornered me after lunch and beat me into a pulp – well, I tried to give back as good as I got, but I was four and they were seven or eight, not to mention there were five of them – how much could I do? The warden was furious and grounded them for several months, while I ended up at a hospital for a few weeks. That's where I met Big Brother for the first time. He had just turned ten, and he was visiting the hospital (it was a charitable hospital) to distribute food packets. Mum and Dad are quite socially responsible that way. We all visit a few institutions on our birthdays and give out food and other stuff – and Mum and Dad also add a big cheque.

So, I was lying in bed wrapped up in bandages like a mummy, trying to grab a fat book left by one of the nurses on the side table. (It was Leo Tolstoy's "War and Peace".) I was frustrated, because my arms weren't long enough to reach the book and I couldn't move my body, but I really needed something to do because I was bored.

"Oh, did you want to read the book?" a soft voice said from the doorway.

I squinted and peered at the beautiful boy entering the room with a basketful of goodies that smelled so good that my stomach rumbled involuntarily. The boy looked about four or five years older than me. He was clean, well-dressed and good-looking. Clearly a well-loved child from an affluent family, I thought enviously.

I really didn't want to antagonise the boy – perhaps he would share some of the heavenly things in his basket with me if he liked me? Encouraged by that thought, I decided I'd pretend to be as normal as I could. So I shook my head and replied, "I just wanted to look at the pictures."

The boy blinked innocently, suddenly looking much younger. His bright blue eyes were really clear, I thought.

"That edition of War and Peace doesn't have any illustrations," he said.

"Oh," I said, taken aback. "You've read it?"

He nodded happily. "I was about your age when I read it," he told me. "How old are you? Three?"

"I'm nearly five!" I blurted out indignantly before I could stop myself.

The boy chuckled. "I'm sorry," he said cheerfully, not looking sorry at all. "Would you like to eat something?" He put the basket on my bed and went to check the patient notes clipped to the bed. He frowned as he read it.

I eyed the basket longingly, not daring to touch it.

The boy picked out several things from the basket and deposited them next to my pillow. "These will not interfere with your treatment," he said gently. "I'll come back with more later if you like them." He smiled at me. "Go on, try one."

I picked up a cupcake and bit into it. It was undoubtedly the best thing I'd ever tasted in my short life.

"It's delicious," I told him. "Thank you."

He beamed at me. "I helped Mum make it," he said proudly. "I figured out the perfect proportion of flour, butter, sugar, eggs and chocolate chips."

"That's really cool," I said admiringly. "You must be a genius."

He nodded. "I am," he said, perfectly naturally. "You're one, too, aren't you?"

I froze.

The boy narrowed his eyes. "Did being smart get you into trouble?" he asked gently.

I nodded silently, wondering if I'd found a kindred soul.

His eyes dimmed. "I used to be called a changeling and a demon child by my biological relatives before I was adopted by Mum and Dad," he said quietly. "My mother died in childbirth, so my father hated me. My grandmother and uncles kept me until I was five. I was so troublesome that they had to keep me chained to a post. If I behaved, they locked me in the study room. I liked that. Books are nice." He smiled slightly.

I reached out and patted his hand comfortingly. (To be honest, I found it strange that the boy would spill out his story to someone he'd just met – much later, he told me once that he'd felt an instant connection with me. Well, he *is* a very trusting person in general, but he rarely divulges his secrets like this – I figure I'm special.)

He brightened immediately and ruffled my hair. I smiled back. We chatted amicably for a while, and I realised that this boy was way cleverer than myself. It made me feel rather happy.

It was only after a well-dressed couple turned up and took him home that I realised I'd forgotten to ask for his name.

I needn't have worried, for he came back the next day with an armful of goodies, toys and books. The couple from the previous day dropped him off and introduced themselves as his parents. They were nice. They were both doctors, but spent most of their time running their family business. They had spoken to my attending doctor and confirmed that the boy's food suggestions from earlier was indeed correct. They seemed so proud of him. Their eyes were soft and gentle as they regarded him. He couldn't see it because he was setting out the stuff for me on the side table, but I could clearly see it. This boy was loved very much by his adoptive parents, just the way proper, real parents should. I felt envy bite at my heart again.

But I forgot about it soon enough – the boy was so charming and smart and innocent that I came to adore him. (I still adore him.) He visited me every day after school, and he always brought good food and fun things with him. With him, I didn't have to hide that I was clever; I couldn't even catch up to him. He taught me so much. I admired him immensely – he was my new hero. I wished he was my big brother. The desire crept in and took over my heart before I knew it. I had even started calling him Big Brother in my head.

The rest of my hospital stay was the brightest period of my short life. I dreaded the day I'd have to return to the orphanage, for my time with Big

Brother would come to an end then. I considered faking an illness to prolong my stay, but I doubted the doctors would be fooled by a nearly five-year-old. Speaking of which, my official birthday was around the corner. In reality, I was already five – I was an abandoned baby, and the warden had put down the day she found me as my birthday. But I was probably already a few weeks old by then. Anyway, no matter the actual date, a birthday was important in the orphanage. We'd get a small gift and a bar of chocolate, and the rest of the kids would sing the birthday song. Normally, I'd have looked forward to it, but this time, all I wanted was to spend more time with my new friend.

Finally, my younger self couldn't hold back anymore. When I learnt that I was going to be discharged in a couple of days, I found myself asking him if he would visit me at the orphanage when I returned.

He looked at me with all the gravity a ten-year-old could muster. "Seccy, do you like living at the orphanage?" he asked.

I shrugged. It was all I had ever known – like or dislike didn't factor into it. I said as much.

He smiled slightly. Later, I would learn that this particular smile was meant to hide his nervousness. "Seccy, I…I feel like you're my little brother. I don't want you to return to the orphanage. I want you to come home with me and be my brother for real." His cheeks were flushed and his eyes were very gentle. "But that's just me. You must tell me what you think. Would you…would you like to be adopted? To be my family?"

I stared at him in shock. My face must have looked awful, for he hurried to add, "It's perfectly fine if you don't want to. I'll always be your friend, and I'll visit you at the orphanage, too."

I grabbed his hands and shook my head fiercely. "No, I don't want to go back," I shouted. "I want to be your brother!"

I never did return to the orphanage. Two days later, on my official birthday, I was discharged from the hospital and taken home by my new family. It was the best birthday ever.

The brilliant, beautiful boy who shone like the sun – that was my Big Brother. Tell me, can any child compete with that? Would any parent ever use him as an example and tell their kids to achieve what he did? Not unless they were clinically insane. And thankfully, most parents are not. Well, at least I like to think so.

I do understand that just because I got lucky enough to be adopted into this lovely family – everyone isn't as fortunate.

4 COURTESY

Courtesy (*noun*):
Polite behaviour – when people are well-spoken, well-mannered, appropriately respectful and follow etiquette.
Example: Oh, that boy greeted all the elders so well, what a courteous child.

***

It is important for a SEC to be courteous. No one wants their own kid to be an ill-mannered rogue – so polite behaviour is as important as being brilliant or winning prizes. Of course, you also need to be the right amount of polite – being overly servile is as bad as being unnecessarily rude. One should be respectful, but not fawning. And it's best to avoid any sort of hypocrisy, sycophancy or falsity as much as possible. Sarcasm could also be offensive, so it's best to keep it limited – although innocuous or self-deprecating sarcasm can be quite beneficial to a conversation at times. It's best to be as real as possible. As Mum says – false modesty is as bad as false praise or false bragging.

I'm quite proud of this, actually. I'm the most courteous person in the family. Big Brother is too innocent and blunt, while Little Sister is rather sarcastic. (It's a different matter that half her sarcasm flies over the heads of the intended targets and they think she's an angel incarnate until they have the misfortune of getting caught in one of her temper tantrums – but that's a different story. She's the youngest, so naturally, we all dote on her and she's a bit of a spoilt brat.)

There was this time when Mum and Dad had taken us to a business dinner party. It was soon after the establishment of my company – they thought it'd be a good idea for all three of us to learn some networking skills. So, off we went to a high-brow party filled with the who's who of our society.

Now, let me tell you – Big Brother and Little Sister are fawned over and practically *worshipped* by people. Plus, both my siblings are trouble-magnets. And all three of us tend to be rather over-protective of each other. Ergo – we stick together in unfamiliar environments, until we find our own circle/people to talk to. Soon enough, we were surrounded by a mixed crowd – ladies mooning over Big Brother and giving vapid, flirty smiles at his blunt responses (he doesn't have much patience with pretentious or dumb people – I didn't realise it for a long time because he was so gentle with the family – but then, all of us *are* really smart, so…), boys falling at Little Sister's feet to gain one haughty, disdainful look from her (seriously, why do my siblings *always* draw the wrong sort of people towards themselves?! Is it too much to ask for a couple of decent humans to fall in love with my precious, precocious siblings?!) – and me, with the older crowd chatting with me with fond, benevolent looks. I've always been popular with the older generation – I didn't understand why for quite some time. Later on, I realised it was simply because I was courteous. It doesn't take much effort to be polite to people, and indifference can be disguised as courtesy very easily. My otherwise brilliant siblings somehow never understood this, despite my attempts to elucidate. Or maybe they just don't want to. That kind of genius comes with its own set of quirks.

So, I was engaged in a pleasant conversation with an influential couple for a bit (and snagged an excellent business deal for my fledgling company), when a loud crash drew everyone's attention. A middle-aged guy – let's call him Mr. Randy (he was an extremely undesirable character: lecherous, disgusting and slimy as hell) – sat on the floor looking dazed, dripping wet. Little Sister stood over him with an upturned glass of lemonade. I spotted Big Brother storming over to her, looking murderous.

Instantly, I knew what must have happened. Mr. Randy had tried to make advances to my Little Sister, and she had shoved him away. Now, she's always been very strong, so it was unsurprising that Mr. Randy had fallen hard, and it looked like he'd sprained an ankle. Good, I thought viciously, but maintained an impassive face as I strode over.

"What happened?" someone asked.

"That rude kid broke my foot!" Mr. Randy howled, pointing at Little Sister.

"That's not all I can break," Little Sister said dangerously. But she was only ten, and she looked cute instead of menacing. "Do you want to try again?" she asked.

Mr. Randy bellowed angrily. Big Brother put an arm around Little Sister's shoulders and pulled her to himself protectively. Both of them wore identical looks of wrath.

The situation, however, was rather tricky. Much as I'd have liked to, this was neither the appropriate venue nor time to beat Mr. Randy into a pulp, even if he fully deserved it. I looked around and found Mum and Dad making their way towards us hurriedly.

Dad and I made eye contact, and I nodded at him. He picked up my cue and quickly ushered Big Brother and Little Sister away. Mum came over to me.

"Could you tell us what happened?" I asked a boy standing nearby. He was clearly one of Little Sister's devotees.

"This man, he – he – he tried to touch her!" the boy said indignantly. Several others around him nodded fervently.

A horrified gasp went through the assembled crowd. This despicable man had actually tried to lay his hands on a child!

"That's not true!" Mr. Randy shouted. "That stupid kid is lying!"

I stepped forward. "Mr. Randy," I asked politely. "Why don't we discuss this like civilised people?" I asked a waiter to help the man to a chair. (It's not that I wanted him to be comfortable – it's just courtesy. And courtesy also wins sympathy from the audience, you know? If we'd left him on the floor like a pitiful creature, someone or the other would have taken his side out of pity.)

Mr. Randy looked a little relieved. "I thought she was a cute kid, reminded me of my own daughter when she was young. I just wanted to speak to her," he grumbled.

"Oh, I see," I said. "My Little Sister is indeed rather pretty. She's only ten, but she's already so beautiful. Maybe in another six or seven years, she'll be a world class beauty."

"Oh yeah," Mr. Randy said, his eyes turning lustful.

It was disgusting. I was very tempted to leave an imprint of my shoe on his gross face. But we needed a better solution.

"How did you approach my sister?" I asked, instead, keeping my voice level and polite.

"I reached out to grab her shoulder," he replied. "She turned around like a frightened duckling."

"She was afraid?" I asked.

"Oh yeah, she looked downright cute, with her big round eyes and smooth skin like butter – just makes you wanna touch and possess..." he said dreamily.

"Is that so?" I couldn't help a tinge of fury leaking into my voice.

"Damn right, she's a doll, that one."

"And you didn't want to wait until she was an adult?"

"Too long a wait," he grumbled.

Mum grabbed my hand. I could feel her shivering. I was equally repulsed. How dare this swine set his filthy sight upon my Little Sister?!

"Mr. Randy, I'm afraid you're going to jail for a long, long time," I said quietly. I turned to the hostess of the party. "Auntie, could you please call the police?" I noticed the hesitation in her eyes. "Please," I added quickly. "I wouldn't want him to molest other children. Your daughters are really pretty, too."

The hostess went pale and immediately called the police. I handed over the recording of our conversation, where Mr. Randy had pretty much confessed to his crime. Little Sister's devotees were more than happy to testify. Many people at the party – especially those with attractive children – promptly hired detectives to investigate Mr. Randy's sordid affairs. By the time he was brought to trial, the incriminating evidence was piled so high that Mr. Randy ended up spending the rest of his life in jail.

See what a bit of courtesy can get you? Now you know why it's an important quality for a SEC.

5 DILIGENT

Diligence (*adjective*):

Careful, hard-working, honest – someone who performs their assigned task properly with great care and attention to detail.

Example: Oh, she even indexed all the references I asked her to check; what a diligent girl!

***

Oh, this one's easy. Everyone loves a hard-working fellow. In fact, one of the first things I learnt from Mum and our HR Head was that we should hire people who are diligent even if they're not as smart as their rival, rather than a smart but lazy person. As is famously attributed to Einstein – genius is 99% diligence and 1% intelligence. Of course, sometimes there are people who defy these odds – but let me tell you, even the most brilliant and talented people will end up with atrophied brains if they don't use it, just like your body will eventually become unable to move if you become too used to a sedentary lifestyle.

Of course, there's the fact that with such extraordinary siblings, I was motivated to work hard to catch up – not that real catching up would ever happen. But you don't want to look like an idiot in front of people you really love (and look up to), right?

And that's pretty much why I've always been a diligent kid. Always did my homework, always did the extra credit assignments, always volunteered to win those brownie points. Also – being diligent has helped me more than I can say when it comes to business.

Besides, it's not like Big Brother and Little Sister don't work hard, because they do. How would they continue to shine so bright if they didn't keep polishing themselves? Even the brightest diamond needs to be cut, and even the brightest metal needs to be polished, right?

However, the results of their hard work versus my hard work – that's barely comparable. And the results of their hard work versus normal people's hard work is…well, to call it a catastrophe wouldn't be an exaggeration. It's like the difference between a brand new luxury cruiser ship and a battered, leaky one-person wooden boat. But between my hard work and an ordinary person's hard work – the difference isn't as stark. In fact, it's not particularly difficult to catch up with me – quite a few of my friends have done so. They often blame their parents' goading, but look – it works!

Like that time when we went to learn ice-skating. Big Brother took one look at the skaters and decided it wasn't his cup of tea. Little Sister took to it like a fish to water (within six months, she had surpassed her instructor, who was a professional, by the way). Me, on the other hand – I was quite eager to learn. I'd learnt ballroom dancing and soccer by then, and I was fairly decent at both. This elegant sport seemed rather attractive to me.

The first week was an unmitigated disaster. I couldn't keep my balance for more than a minute. (Little Sister was already circling the rink expertly by then.) I was frozen half to death and full of bruises – and really, really disheartened. (Cut me some slack, I was only twelve.)

That weekend, Mum and Dad watched me anxiously at dinner, their concern-filled gazes filling me with warmth and shame simultaneously. Couldn't I even do something as simple as ice-skating properly, I asked myself. I lost my appetite and excused myself from the dinner table.

I went to my room and was about to slam the door shut when Dad appeared.

"Seccy," he said softly. "Are you feeling unwell?"

I shook my head.

Gentle hands rubbed my hair and checked my forehead for fever. Perhaps it's because they are doctors, but both Mum and Dad have very gentle hands. They make you feel so warm and comfortable and wrapped in kindness that you melt.

Dad frowned. "You have a light fever," he said. "Come, I'll prepare some soup for you."

"It's fine, Dad," I told him. "I'm not very hungry."

"It's not good for a growing child to miss his meals," he said, patting my shoulder. "Come along, child."

I winced slightly. I *was* bruised all over (and desperate to keep it from my parents, for I knew they'd worry unnecessarily).

Of course, you can't escape a parent's eye.

Dad knelt on the floor and looked into my eyes, his expression very serious. "Seccy," he said, his deep voice a comforting rumble. "Are you injured?"

"Not really," I mumbled. "Just a few bruises. I'll be fine by tomorrow morning."

You know how I said before that we siblings are rather overprotective? We learnt it from our parents. Not even a single papercut would be ignored in the family. It's not like they'd make a huge fuss over it or prevent us from doing what we wanted – I did learn fencing later, and my Little Sister is a certified trainer for six types of adventure sports – it was just that they took our well-being (both physical and mental) very, very seriously.

Dad's frown deepened. "Show me."

I shook my head. I knew I would be in trouble as soon as he saw the bruises.

"Seccy," Dad said, his voice deceptively soft but full of threat. "Don't make me call Mum."

Ouch. Evading one of them was difficult enough…evading both of them? Impossible. Utterly, absolutely impossible. Even Little Sister can't stand up to that, let alone me or Big Brother.

I caved. Dad hissed angrily when he saw the bruises. "What on earth is your instructor doing, letting you get injured like this?! I'm definitely speaking with him tomorrow."

Actually, it wasn't really the instructor's fault. I was just…over enthusiastic. I said as much, but Dad ignored me. He patched me up quickly, expertly and I felt much better. Then he bundled me into bed and went to fetch soup.

I was forbidden from going out the next day. Mum made my favourite breakfast. After Mum and Dad left for work, Big Brother and Little Sister came to my room.

I was quite surprised. Why hadn't Little Sister gone for her practice?

"She wanted to stay with you," Big Brother said helpfully at my questioning look.

Little Sister glared at him. Then she looked at me. "You have to change your instructor – this one's no good."

I shrugged. He was the one assigned to my group – and I didn't think he was particularly bad or anything.

"You don't have to ice-skate if you don't want to," Big Brother declared. "It's a waste of your time and talent. It's only for nimble little monkeys like this one," he said, rubbing Little Sister's hair.

I giggled at her aggrieved look.

"Brother Seccy is not a lazy bum like you," she snapped at Big Brother. "He can definitely ice-skate properly – he just needs a decent teacher." Her eyes sparkled as she looked at me. "Do you want me to teach you? I can't do any fancy stuff yet, but I can definitely teach you to circle around the rink without falling!"

"Sure," I said. She'd definitely have some useful pointers.

Little Sister rubbed her hands gleefully. "Stand up!" she ordered.

"Hold on," Big Brother protested. "He's still ill."

"I'm fine," I said, and stood up.

Over the next two hours, Little Sister corrected my postures and gave me tips and tricks and a fair bit of basic information which I hadn't known before. Perhaps my instructor had forgotten a few essential things, I conceded.

Thanks to Little Sister, I was able to move around without falling soon enough. Mum and Dad also found a new instructor for me. Little Sister and her award-winning instructor quizzed him before he was finally allowed to teach me.

Three months later, Little Sister needed a partner to enter a competition, and insisted I accompany her on the ice. I can happily say that I didn't embarrass her. My hard work did pay off. Little Sister won all the individual performances, naturally – and for the paired performance, we got third place. I was rather apologetic for dragging her down, but she seemed quite pleased and told me that if it had been anyone else but me, they wouldn't even have made it to the semi-finals.

Well, at least all the secret practice paid off. My instructor was quite pleased, too – for he suddenly got a bunch of new students...mostly my friends and acquaintances. One of them even went on to become a professional later on – and he's the one that accompanies Little Sister when she needs a partner these days.

6 EFFECTIVE

Effective (*adjective*):
Doing what you're supposed to do and achieving the desired/intended result.
Example: To be effective, I need to finish three assignments today.

***

The world is all about results, isn't it? If one doesn't have "goal-oriented" or "result-oriented" on their CV these days…well, goodbye prospective new job! Quite contradictory to ancient teachings, which tell you to fulfil your duties and perform your tasks and not worry about the results.

Anyway, the thing is, a SEC needs to be effective. If homework is to be submitted on Friday, a SEC must submit it on Friday, or the SEC loses his/her effectiveness. Besides, keeping deadlines is a skill which works well in the long run, especially in the business world. I'm very proud to say that I've never missed a deadline. And I'm definitely a success story, if nothing else!

It's not particularly difficult to be effective. One just needs to stick to the plan and do things the way they're supposed to be done. Of course, if you procrastinate on one part, you have to work extra on the other parts to make up for it. But still, it's doable. (That I admit having done…pushed things away until the last minute.)

The trick about putting things off until the last minute is knowing your own capacity and capability…and figuring out the required task and the approximate time it'd need. If you have no clue about something, it's better to start early (I often do this). However, if you know what you have to do and how to do it, you can afford to laze around for a bit (*modus operandi* of

Little Sister in general, though I do this at times, too). The absolute fool proof way to be effective and still laze around is to finish off quickly and then vegetate (Big Brother's preferred method, and sometimes I do this, too). That's the secret to keeping to deadlines and being effective. Gosh, I should sell this as a management trick, right? Maybe I can get an award. My award corner is looking a bit deserted these days.

There are many self-help books which teach you how to be effective. It's one of the buzz-words these days. The good thing is, this is one of the easiest things to be. Most tasks come with a range approximation, so that makes it easy to accomplish. It is important to remember what the intended result is, though. Yup, that's of paramount importance. It doesn't matter how smart or skilled or amazing you are if you can't achieve the required result. On the other hand, it also doesn't matter how dull or boring or unskilled you are if you are an effective person. People who can deliver results are always in demand, even if their other attributes are less than desirable — especially the ones who achieve exactly what was intended, and neither over-perform nor under-perform.

I like to think that I'm pretty decent at this. Others don't always agree. Just the other day, when conducting an inspection of one of the associate companies, I found a slight discrepancy in the finished product and the given specifications — the manufactured product was standard sized, while the specifications requested by the client was marginally different. I sent the entire batch for reprocessing. Thankfully, we had enough time to do it over. The production team (headed by one of Dad's cousins) was quite unhappy and went to complain to Dad, saying such a small difference would never be noticed by the customer, and wouldn't impact use of the product at all — and how I'd unnecessarily incurred a huge cost for the company.

Dad being Dad, called over everyone and told me to explain my actions — giving me a chance to show off. I did so, naturally.

There were two happy consequences of this event — first, the client was super-happy with our product, because he'd been to a lot of people and everyone ended up giving him the standard sized stuff like the batch I discarded. Second, a lot of people in our group pulled up their socks and got serious about their work. Performance levels are looking up already, and it's been only a few weeks.

7 FASTIDIOUS

Fastidious (*adjective*):
Someone who attaches great importance to cleanliness, even the smaller details. The "neat-freaks", in popular language.
Example: She keeps her floors so clean that you can eat off them.

***

If someone tells me they don't like clean people, I'm not going to believe that. Ever. Even the sloppiest person would prefer a clean person over another sloppy person. It's human nature. No one wants a hair in their soup, after all. In fact, from what I've seen, it's the slobs who like neat-freaks the most, because then these neat-freaks will compulsively clean up the slob's mess.

This characteristic is most relevant and most often used as an example by parents/guardians of teenagers. That's what I've been told, at least.

Now – let me make it very clear that being a fastidious person does not mean that one is suffering from obsessive compulsive disorder. Some people like to keep themselves and their surroundings clean. It is an attractive trait, although rarer than I'd like it to be.

Children, in general, are also less concerned about cleanliness than adults – and thus, a clean, well-groomed child immediately gets ranked highly on the SEC scale. In fact, this is one of the areas where I'd have won many points, even as a child. I like things to be clean; I always have, even when I was small. And clean as in properly clean, not "shove them under the bed and forget about them" kind of clean.

The primary reason for my fastidiousness is a well-kept secret – I can't stand bugs. Now, as a functional adult male, it is rather embarrassing for me to admit in public that I'm terrified of anything that crawls. So it is hidden under the garb of fastidiousness. After all, if everything is sparkling clean, there's no chance of creepy-crawlies sneaking in, right? Well, mostly.

Once, Little Sister had coerced us all into going camping in the woods for her birthday. I don't like camping. At all. There are too many crawling and flying things…and apparently, my blood is the equivalent of thirty-year-old scotch for mosquitoes and other blood-sucking bugs. It's a nightmare.

Big Brother doesn't like camping, either. Unfamiliar bedding, unfamiliar scents and sounds – he's sensitive to these. He's not as squeamish as I am, though.

Mum and Dad are pretty neutral, and they were quite ok with the whole idea.

But Little Sister really, really wanted to go camping with the family, so none of us had the heart to refuse her.

So we went. We set up the tents, made a bonfire, roasted sausages and potatoes and marshmallows. I slathered myself in insect-repellent lotions, I'd have bundled myself up if it hadn't been so warm outside. To her credit, Little Sister did ensure that the place would be as bug-free as possible.

Unfortunately, when it comes to man versus nature, nature will inevitably win.

Thus, in the middle of the night, a creeping sensation on my arm woke me up. (Normally, I sleep like a log – but when you're scared, your sleep gets lighter, so…) I was scared stiff.

"Dad…Big Brother…" I whispered pitifully, not even daring to open my mouth to scream.

Fortunately, doctors have this almost supernatural ability to sense distress.

"Seccy?" Dad's sleepy but gentle voice asked. "What's wrong, son?"

"There's something on my arm. It crawls…" I whispered.

"I'll get it," Dad said. "Don't move, ok?"

"Ok," I replied weakly.

Dad switched on a flashlight and swept the thing off my arm with a handkerchief. He checked my arm for bites or allergies first, and then went to check on the thing he'd flung aside.

By now, Big Brother had woken up, too.

"What's going on?" he mumbled sleepily, opening one eye.

Then, probably at the distressed look on my face, he sat up abruptly, looking alarmed.

"Seccy? What happened?" he asked solicitously.

"Something crawled up my arm…" I told him.

"It's a centipede," Dad said. "A harmless one, though, thankfully."

Big Brother peered at the squiggly black thing Dad held in the handkerchief.

I couldn't hold it in anymore. I screamed.

Mum and Little Sister came over from the other tent immediately.

"What happened?" Mum asked.

Little Sister spotted the monster in Dad's hand and squealed excitedly. She actually *likes* bugs, can you believe that?!

"Where did you find it?" she asked excitedly. "Are there more?"

The thought of more of these things crawling around in the tent was the final straw for me. Blessed darkness took me away and when I regained consciousness, I was back home, in my own clean, safe, bug-free bed.

8 GENIAL

Genial (*adjective*):
Friendly and cheerful – in a nice way, not in a creepy way.
Example: His genial approach to troubled persons made him an extraordinary coach.

***

Friendly and cheerful – it's easy, isn't it? Who would want to hold up a dark, gloomy, taciturn character as an example?

One doesn't necessarily need to be an extrovert or an excessively social person. All of us have friends who are somewhat reserved and shy, but have a pleasant, cheerful personality. Being cheerful also doesn't mean that you have to be constantly smiling – that'd be highly abnormal. Everyone has their highs and lows – it's just about how you present yourself to the world. A general positive attitude is good, and geniality usually comes automatically with it. And sometimes, it can bring you the best of friends.

Yup, happened with me.

In fact, the very first day of school after being adopted – I was trundling behind Big Brother like a lost little duckling until he brought me to my class. Then he knelt and cupped my face in his bigger hands.

"Seccy," he said seriously. "This is your classroom. Here's where you will spend a whole year, and here's where you will make new friends. Don't be afraid. You're nice and smart – they're going to love you. Just be yourself, all right?"

I nodded tearfully.

"Go in, introduce yourself and speak to other kids your age. Oh, and your assigned desk will have your name on it, you can put down your bag there," Big Brother said. "When the bell rings, it'll be time for the morning assembly – that happens there." He pointed at the assembly hall he'd shown me earlier. "So all of you will have to go there, ok?"

I nodded again.

Big Brother ruffled my hair. "Good boy," he said. "I'll come and meet you here at lunch." He kissed my brow, just like Mum and Dad had done in the morning. "Good luck, Seccy."

I watched his back until I could no longer see him. Then, swallowing my anxiety, I entered the room.

Several faces as nervous as myself looked up at me. I was relieved not to be the only anxious one.

I smiled and waved my hand. "Good morning. I'm Seccy," I announced.

A lot of people smiled and waved back. I looked around and found my desk. It was a nice spot by the window. Pleased, I put down my bag and smiled at the boy sitting behind me.

"Hello," I said.

He nodded, but didn't smile or say anything.

"I'm Seccy," I said, holding out my hand. I'd seen Mum and Dad do this when they met new people.

The boy looked rather stunned. Then he smiled shyly and shook hands with me. "I'm Bestie," he said quietly.

"Pleased to meet you, Bestie," I said cheerfully.

Then I waved at the girl sitting behind him. Then the kids sitting next to us. By the time the bell rang do the assembly, there were seven of us.

That was twenty years ago. The seven of us are the best of friends – almost as close as siblings – even now.

You see, people can be divided into various categories. Let me explain using concentric circles. If we make a big circle – that'll be all the people in the world. Then a smaller circle inside it – that'll be people we've met. Then a smaller one within it – that'll be our acquaintances – that's people we know reasonably well (as opposed to people we've met but not really interacted with). Within the acquaintances circle, we'll have a smaller circle – our friends and extended family. Within this, we'll have an even smaller circle – close family and friends – the people dearest to us. Sometimes, some people – when they've found true love – have another circle inside this that contains just that one special person – like Mum and Dad have each other. I haven't gotten there yet.

9 HEARTY

Hearty (*adjective*):

Strong and healthy, robust – also enthusiastic – basically someone brimming with life.

Example: From his rosy cheeks, cheerful manner and booming laugh, it was easy to know what a hearty person he was.

***

This is a tricky one. It's not absolutely essential for a SEC to be in the peak of health or to be a big, strong person, to be honest. Plenty of people with diminutive frames are on top of the SEC list…other characteristics matter more.

However, it is helpful to be hale and hearty. Everyone likes a lively person. Besides, all those grand achievements and exemplary conduct can be quite taxing, so health is a concern. Also, since versatility is a factor – if you want to do different things and present yourself as a multi-talented person, you'd have to be reasonably strong and sturdy. I know of some people who think it's fashionable to be frail and delicate – but honestly, I'm not sure that's a good line of thought. There was a period of time in the middle where I was rather sickly myself – and it was horrible. Fortunately, I recovered fully – but there are people who want to be healthy but can't be…so it somewhat annoys me when I see perfectly healthy people ruining their health for stupid reasons. The old adage – health is wealth – is not wrong.

A person brimming with life will naturally have a positive attitude. Just look at Little Sister. She's the liveliest, heartiest person I know. And despite her penchant for adventure sports and honing her fighting skills, she takes very good care of herself. You should see how disciplined her schedule is.

She's the poster girl for healthy. How else would she be able to throw herself off planes and cliffs for fun? You need a strong, healthy body for these things.

The rough patch I spoke of happened when I was seventeen. Growing up around doctors – even if they're not practising ones – makes one naturally sensitive to bodily anomalies. So, when I felt unwell and my intuition felt as if something was seriously wrong, I went to my parents. I was right to be suspicious. It was an early stage of leukaemia. Since it was detected early, I recovered fully in a few months – but those months were gruelling. I'd always taken my health as a matter of course – it had never occurred to me before this that I could be seriously ill at some point. It was difficult, those months. I tried to be as cheerful as I could, and the unflinching support from my family and friends made a world of difference…but sometimes, in the early hours, I would wonder if I was really getting better, or just moving slowly but surely towards an early death…if I'd even live past my twentieth birthday.

Fortunately, I made a full recovery, and I've had no recurrence till date. I did learn an important lesson, though…and my gratitude at having survived gave me a much more positive outlook than before. I still remember the day I left the hospital after being declared cancer-free. The sun shone brighter, the sky looked prettier, the smiling faces of my family looked more precious than ever before. I couldn't stop smiling all the way home…and for several days after that. Life and health are something one truly needs to cherish.

10 INDEPENDENT

Independent (*adjective*):
Self-reliant, not dependant – I'm talking about the general attitude here, not monetary support.
Example: She is very capable and independent; she can even finish the entire task by herself.

***

Our parents brought us up to be independent (yes, despite all the overprotectiveness and pampering) – it was the one thing they always laid great emphasis on. It is an essential survival skill to be able to do things for yourself – you may not need to on a regular basis, but you never know when there could be an emergency and you'd need to survive that. Being dysfunctional was never an option for us. Yes, even Big Brother with his negligible life-skills and me with my squeamishness can live by ourselves – and live decently, like a proper human, not a half-zombie.

This is important for a SEC, too – for a SEC typically demonstrates leadership skills. And it is important for a leader to be independent. To take initiative. To be able to take decisions. They tell you all this in the fancy leadership training sessions these days. I speak in those at times, too. Pretty cool, eh?

Sometimes, being independent can also get you into trouble, though. The whole morality-ethics-rules entanglement. You break a rule to do something you feel is right – or maybe because you had no other option. I've done both, and I've been praised and reprimanded for both.

Like that time in B-school, when Bestie and I broke curfew (and probably a dozen other hostel rules) to prevent a suicidal classmate from killing himself. The guy had been depressed for a while – his girlfriend dumped him, his grades were low, his parents were being too strict – there was a long story behind it. The guy didn't even want to be in B-school – his passion lay in painting. And he did paint beautifully; we all loved his art. It was fascinating to watch him paint, too. His normal gloomy countenance would light up and there'd be a gentle smile on his face. He was a decent guy overall, and while he was a little reserved, he did hang out with his classmates.

So, one evening, when he didn't turn up for a class meeting, alarm bells rang in our heads. His roommate said that he'd received a letter from his father in the morning and he'd been down in the dumps since then. We all split up into smaller groups to look for him – but we were unable find him anywhere in the hostel. We needed to look outside, so a couple of boys went to the warden to update him about the situation.

That's when Bestie spotted something unusual on the roof of the library building. We exchanged a horrified look as soon as we figured out what it was. Then, without wasting a second, the two of us ran out. We skipped over the hostel gates, broke into the library building and ran to the roof, barely in time to pull the guy off the parapet.

He was sent to a therapist, and we were grounded for a week – but we were also given medals for rescuing a fellow student.

Was it a surprise that Bestie and I won the next student elections by a landslide?

Later on, the boy's parents came to speak to Bestie and I. They thanked us for saving their son, and informed us that he was withdrawing from B-school and going to art school instead.

Today, he is one of the most celebrated artists in the country. Bestie and I receive a painting from him each year on our birthdays – thanks to him, our art collection is already worth millions, and continues to grow rapidly.

11 JUDICIOUS

Judicious (*adjective*):
Having good judgement – capable of making solid decisions. There's an element of rationality as well as prudence involved.
Example: Not marrying a person with loose morals is a judicious choice.

***

It is important for a SEC to be able to choose well. The ability to take good, solid decisions, to act reasonably, logically, prudently – those are the cornerstone for success, and what's a SEC without success?

Decision-making is not an easy or a simple task. One needs to analyse a lot of things – right from the causes to the choices to the consequences. Sometimes, one needs to act to achieve the best possible outcome rather than the perfect outcome where everyone is happy. In fact, real life is rarely so neat as to allow a perfect outcome. So, one needs to be judicious to be able to determine what to hold on to and what to leave behind. This applies to small, everyday things as well as big, life-and-death decisions.

That reminds me of this time when an old enemy of Dad's nearly got us killed. So, Dad's from this super-old, blue-blooded family, right? They do a lot of things traditionally, like determining the heir of the next generation (who goes on to become the head of the family once the previous head steps down or reaches the age of sixty, whichever is earlier) and all. Some of their traditions are antediluvian, while some are surprisingly modern. Like the heir can only be a person with the surname of the main family branch and a child that has been raised by a member of the main branch for at least ten years – but this child need not be a blood relative; an adopted kid who can demonstrate their talent is a perfectly viable candidate – plus, it's gender-neutral, with the only caveat being that the female heir must retain her surname when she gets married, and if she intends to raise any of her children as a prospective heir, that child should have the surname as well.

It's fairly common in these big, rich families to have disputes over the choice of an heir (it's like selecting a crown prince – and if you think that sounds dramatic, you have to attend one of the all-family annual gatherings; let me tell you – reality shows have nothing on the drama our extended family is capable of enacting!) and division of property and tasks and so on – sometimes it can get really vicious.

Dad was chosen to be the next heir when he was twenty-two. Grandfather once told us that there was fierce competition, but Dad won in the end. The selection process is actually a series of tests measuring intelligence, physical strength, business acumen, communication skills, problem-solving skills, personality type and so on. It's like a super-tough entrance exam. Once top three candidates have been shortlisted, the elders (anyone over sixty) cast their votes. The presiding head has a veto power as well as a decisive vote in case there's a tie or he deems the candidate with majority votes to be unsuitable. So Dad and another heir candidate – let's call him Uncle Crazy (he really is crazy) – were neck to neck for the top spot, while candidate #3 was far behind. The presiding head – let's call him Great-Uncle Rich – is actually Uncle Crazy's father. However, he cast his vote in Dad's favour, saying he was more suitable than Uncle Crazy. Well, you can imagine what happened next. Uncle Crazy went berserk, declared that Dad would be his sworn enemy for life and stuff. Great-Aunt Rich pulled him away and took him overseas for half a year to calm him down. Later on, Uncle Crazy and Dad were on civil terms, but there was always this undercurrent of animosity between them.

When Great-Uncle Rich stepped retired from his position, Dad took on the role of the head of the family. The selection process for the next heir began. The eligible age group is sixteen to forty, and *everyone* in the family is supposed to enter, unless they are disabled in some way or incapable of competing. Little Sister had just turned sixteen – so all three of us ended up participating. Uncle Crazy's two kids participated as well.

Now, Big Brother and Little Sister couldn't be more uninterested in being the heir – Big Brother even tried to claim that his staggering intelligence makes him incapable of running a family business to get himself out of the selection process (the elders just laughed it off), while Little Sister spent hours lamenting the fact that she wasn't old enough to get married so she could change her surname and escape. Me, on the other hand…I was interested. I'd been running my company for several years now, and I enjoyed it very much. I'd also seen business decisions being taken at the parent company level which reeked of personal bias, and it grated on my nerves. I'd seen how Mum and Dad had poured their heart and soul into the family business, and I hated it when their efforts were either overlooked or set aside. I also knew that there was some brewing resentment against Mum and Dad, because they are too honest for their own good. They are the type that would rather walk out of a super-profitable deal than besmirch their hands with a little illegality. That rubbed a lot of people the wrong way. I hoped that things would get better with Dad at the helm, but a captain cannot run his ship by himself. He needs good shipmates.

And, more than anything, I *wanted* to work with Dad. I *wanted* to succeed the family business after him. It was a secret dream of mine – like a historical drama in my head – with Dad as the emperor and me as the crown prince. I wanted to be a hero that protected my empire and won over enemies, both internal and external. Of course, I wouldn't dare to say it out loud.

Nonetheless, my family figured it out soon enough, no matter how much I tried to hide my secret ambition. The day before the selection process, Mum and Dad pulled me aside to chat.

"Seccy," Mum said seriously. "Are you interested in being the heir and taking over when Dad steps down?"

I hesitated. After all, I was adopted. There had been only one adopted heir in the glorious five-hundred years of family history…and that one had been an illegitimate child who was adopted later, so he still had blood ties. I, on the other hand, was a complete stranger, and no one even knew where my DNA came from. (I had secretly investigated – it was a dead end.)

"I think you are the most capable one for this position among all the participants," Dad said. "But if you're really not interested, I'll use my veto to get you out."

I stared at my toes. "Do you want me to?" I asked in a small voice.

I could hear them sigh.

"Seccy," Dad said gently. "The biggest pride of a parent is when their child chooses to follow their footsteps. I'd be proud and happy and honoured beyond measure should you choose to follow me."

Mum picked up the thread. "But it's not Dad's decision, my dear boy – it's yours. We want you to do it only if *you* want to do it – not because you think it'd make Dad happy. We want you to be free to live your life the way you want to live, doing what you enjoy. We know you're great at this – but it is more important to us whether you like it or not. We don't want you to feel stifled or push you into doing something you don't want to do."

You know that warm and happy feeling that suddenly expands inside you until you feel ready to burst? I felt like that as I looked up at my parents.

"I want to," I told them honestly. "I've always wanted to. I enjoy business. It's just that I…is it ok for an outsider like me to take on such an important role?"

Mum and Dad were livid.

"Who the hell said you were an outsider?" Dad demanded angrily.

"Tell Mum who told you such a ridiculous thing, baby," Mum said, her voice soft and dangerous. Ouch – that tone of Mum's was the red flag that we were all wary of. This was her Mama Bear mode.

To be honest, there had been a few times when some cousins had mentioned this to me. I don't think it was malicious – not from the cousins' side at least (although the adults around them probably didn't have good intentions) – it was more like, "Oh, you're fun, I like you even though you're an outsider."

I shrugged nonchalantly – I didn't want them worrying over something like this. I wasn't particularly bothered by such comments; I knew I was loved by my parents, and I loved them very much in return. The same went for my siblings. Mum and Dad were the *real* parents to all three of us. Our biological parents – or sperm and egg donators as Little Sister called them – didn't matter. For me, they didn't even exist – and Big Brother and Little Sister hadn't had the best of experiences with theirs.

Dad sighed. "Seccy, who are we to you?" he asked quietly.

Huh, what? I stared at him open-mouthed. What on earth…?! Why did he suddenly look so sad?!

"You're my parents," I said firmly. "My *real* parents."

"If we are your real parents, how can you be an outsider?" Dad asked.

"Did we raise you to be stupid? You're our kid. All three of you are our kids. Who's the outsider here?" Mum burst out.

And just like that, all the hesitation, all the doubts – everything disappeared from my heart. I felt lighter than air.

"Sorry, Mum. Sorry, Dad. I had a stupid moment there," I told him, unable to keep the smile off my face. Who cared about blood? Our bonds were much stronger.

"Good," Mum and Dad said at the same time.

"So, then," Mum continued. "Have you figured out what you want to do?"

I nodded eagerly. "I want to be the heir. I want to follow Dad."

Mum rubbed her hands together gleefully, and Dad looked extremely smug.

"Excellent," they said.

You can probably predict what happened next. Top three? Big Brother, Little Sister and me. (I knew they didn't botch up the tests to ensure that the three of us got to the top three, so that the rest of the family would have no choice other than me – as I've said before, I'm the most popular one with the older generations.) Elders' vote? Me, naturally. (Being a SEC helps.)

And so I became the crown prince.

There was a family gathering after that, and Uncle Crazy walked up to where Dad and I were chatting with Great-Uncle Rich.

"You lucky dog," Uncle Crazy sneered at Dad. "Look at you – proudly showing off three extraordinary kids."

Dad smiled broadly. "Of course. I am very proud of my children. They are magnificent."

"And you even managed to get one of your mongrels to win the heir's role," Uncle Crazy continued.

Dad's face went cold. "What did you just call my son?" he asked dangerously.

Uncle Crazy suddenly whipped out a pistol and aimed it at Dad. "I'll get you today, you bastard! And then I'll kill your mongrel heir, too!"

All of us froze.

"Seccy, get behind me," Dad ordered calmly, trying to shield me.

Out of the corner of my eye, I spotted Little Sister making her way towards us. Relieved, I focussed on Uncle Crazy. And promptly panicked again, because if he fired now, he'd injure Dad very seriously…might even hit a vital spot. I knew I had to act judiciously if Dad and I were to survive this.

"You'll rot in jail for the rest of your life if you did that," I told Uncle Crazy. If I angered him, he'd either shoot immediately and his aim would falter, which would give me enough time to get Dad and me down, or he'd start ranting, which would buy us enough time for Little Sister (and the guards accompanying her) to capture him.

"Shut up!" Uncle Crazy shouted, and fired.

Thanks to his agitation, his aim was off. I tackled Dad to the floor and felt the bullet graze my arm.

The next instant, Uncle Crazy cried out in pain as Little Sister took him down with a beautifully executed flying roundhouse kick. The pistol went flying.

"Awesome," I murmured. Little Sister's skills never failed to amaze me.

"Seccy? Seccy!" Dad's voice was shaking. I'd never heard his voice shake before.

"I'm ok, Dad. It's just a graze," I told him. My arm hurt like hell and I wanted to faint, but Dad's shaking voice made me struggle to keep awake.

Then I felt gentle fingers on my arm and Mum's voice said, "He'll be all right. Calm down, dear."

I also saw Big Brother's fuzzy outline at her shoulder. Assured of our safety, I gave in to the velvety darkness.

When I woke up, I was yelled at for two hours and then grounded for two months. And when I recovered, Little Sister subjected me to physical training straight out of hell because she claimed my reflexes weren't fast enough if I got injured so stupidly. Big Brother shut himself up in one of the company laboratories and came up with a fortified graphene material that would stop a cannonball, let alone a bullet. It won us a ton of military contracts later. Dad threatened to ground me for life if I ever did something like this again.

I put up with it for a while, but I was secretly frustrated. Was it too much to ask for a "well done"? I'd taken the best available option, saved Dad and myself, and gotten off practically unscathed…well, with a minor bullet wound.

Finally, I couldn't take it anymore and grumbled to Mum. She sighed and gave me an are-you-stupid look.

"Seccy – none of us are ever going to praise you for putting yourself at risk," she said finally. "And Dad's mad because it is a parent's prerogative to protect their kids. He feels like he failed you."

I blinked at her in confusion and she chuckled helplessly. "His Papa Bear pride is hurt," she said.

"He shouted at me for being unfilial because I didn't listen to him," I complained. "He told me to get behind him. If I'd done that, Uncle Crazy would have seriously wounded him! Was I supposed to let that happen?"

Mum sighed again. "I don't know," she said. "Logically, what you did was probably right…but I hate that you endangered yourself."

"There was minimal danger," I protested. "I thought it through."

Mum suddenly enveloped me in a hug. "I know," she whispered. "I know you did what you thought best…but we were terrified, Seccy. Our son was hurt…our son exposed himself to harm. What if…what if you got seriously injured?!"

I could feel her trembling. I felt a little guilty. "Mum, I'll be more careful in the future, all right?"

"Promise?" she asked, her eyes shining with unshed tears.

"Promise," I replied.

"Good," she said. "You're still grounded, though."

"Mum!"

12 KINDNESS

Kindness (*noun*):
Being considerate, generous, helpful
Example: The kind pedestrian took the injured dog to the veterinary hospital.

***

Kindness is an underrated virtue in some walks of life, and an overrated one in some others. While it is important for humans – especially a SEC – to be kind, too much kindness (like Big Brother) is troublesome. One must be judicious in their kindness, and one must remember that a bleeding heart is as bad as an unkind person.

Oh, that reminds me – an unkindness of ravens. This collective noun always cracks me up. Who on earth even came up with it? Are ravens unkind birds? I don't think so. Other than humans, other creatures seldom seek to harm or attack unprovoked or unnecessarily. I doubt a group of ravens would be unkind to anyone. A group of humans, on the other hand…I'd be surprised if the degree of unkindness simmering there was low.

Despite that jaded point of view, however, I like to think of myself as a moderately kind person. I'm not extraordinarily considerate, and I am openly generous only to people I like – but it's not like I'd ignore someone in need if I could easily extend a helping hand. My kindness does not extend to activities that would harm my family or friends, though.

Still, this balanced position makes most people think I'm kind. It's usually in the small stuff. Sometimes, though, a small kindness can get you a disproportionately huge reward. This, I can speak from personal experience. Big Brother and I, for a small, kind gesture, reaped the biggest reward of our lives.

It was the summer vacation of my tenth year of existence, and Mum and Dad had taken us to visit Mum's parents – we called them Granny and Gramps – in a small university town. Mum comes from a long line of academics. This side of the family is the opposite of Dad's. Mum's relatives look down on money and prize only academic achievements. Naturally, Big Brother is the apple of their eyes.

Big Brother loved this place, and we often wandered around the town on our own. It was green and hilly and full of libraries and lakes and little groves. Of course, Big Brother loved libraries the most, and I often dragged him out for walks when I felt we'd studied too much.

One evening, we were walking along the hillside on our way back to our grandparents' house, when we came across a fight. It was the most one-sided fight I'd ever seen. A small girl – no more than five or six – was beating up three older kids (two boys and a girl) at least twice her age. In fact, one of the boys looked almost as old as Big Brother.

"Mummy and Daddy will teach you a lesson when we go home, you little shit!" one of the boys yelled, raising his hand to throw a stone at the little girl.

Big Brother and I couldn't ignore this. Three to one is unfair even in a fight among peers, let alone a little girl like this. While she had been dominating the fight till now, we could see that she was getting tired. After all, she was just a small child. I remembered how I'd been beaten up by bullies when I was her age – of course, that had led to me meeting Big Brother and getting adopted, so I wasn't complaining.

Big Brother grabbed the boy's arm before he could throw the stone while I stood protectively in front of the little girl.

"Is there a problem?" Big Brother asked coldly. He can be very intimidating when he chooses to be, although he rarely uses it. Plus, he's always been tall and beautiful.

The two boys stepped back fearfully and the girl blushed, looking at Big Brother with amorous eyes. Ugh.

I stepped forward. "Shame on you, bullying a small child like this," I said, throwing them a disgusted look I learnt from Mum.

The three of them stared at me as if I'd lost my mind.

"How were we bullying her?" the younger boy yelled. "Clearly she was the one beating us up!"

The little girl behind us giggled. "That's right," she said. "Even a five-year-old can beat these idiots even when they gang up on me."

"Despicable," Big Brother spat.

"Now, look here," the oldest boy said. "That rude kid is our freeloading cousin. This is a family matter and you can't interfere. It's our parents that are feeding her!"

Big Brother and I turned to look at the skinny, filthy child behind us.

"Doesn't look like you're feeding her," I remarked.

Their faces turned sour.

"We'll complain to our parents!" the girl threatened.

"Go ahead," I told her.

Big Brother pointed at our grandparents' house. "That's where we're staying," he said. "We are taking her with us. If you want to bring your parents to complain, you are welcome to come over."

"Now scram," I said imperiously. "Or I will show you my taekwondo moves."

"What's that?" the little girl behind us asked curiously.

"It's a great way to beat up people. I can take down ten at a time!" I bragged (untruthfully).

Big Brother gave me a disgruntled look, but the little girl looked awed and delighted. "I wanna learn to!" she said.

She was adorable, I thought.

I turned to the three big kids and raised an eyebrow. "Why are you still here?"

They looked a little doubtful about my tall claims, but they were cowards anyway, so they ran off.

We headed home.

It turned out that Granny and Gramps knew who the little girl was. Her parents had passed away in a car accident last year, and since then, she had been passed around from one relative to another like a rather undesirable package.

A surge of protectiveness welled up in me. I glanced at Big Brother, and he nodded. We had the same thought.

The little girl – Mum had helped her clean up – was currently sitting on the piano bench with Dad and he was showing her how to play a simple tune. She giggled happily and followed his finger movements perfectly.

The rest of us were quite impressed.

Three days later, no one had come to pick up the girl. Our vacation was nearing its end, and we would soon return to the city. We didn't want to leave her behind, though.

"I've always wanted a daughter," Mum muttered. "And the boys adore her."

Dad nodded and looked at Big Brother and me. We wanted her to be our younger sister.

Big Brother glanced at me. "Seccy, you want to ask her?"

I was a little nervous, but I nodded. I wondered if Big Brother had felt like this five years ago when he'd asked me.

I turned to the little girl we'd come to love in three short days. "We will be going back to the city in a few days," I told her.

Her face fell.

"Would you like to come with us? As our little sister?" I added quickly.

Her eyes widened in shock. "You mean…you guys want to…*adopt* me?"

I nodded. "If you're ok with it, we'd really, really like you to be our Little Sister forever."

She threw herself at me and clung to my neck. "I want to!" she cried. "I want to be with Big Brother and Brother Seccy!"

"Excellent," Dad said. "I'll make the arrangements."

So Mum, Dad, Granny and Gramps went off to take care of the legalities and paperwork, while Big Brother, Little Sister and I started making plans on what to do once we went back home.

And that's how a small, random act of kindness got us our precious Little Sister.

Ah, this wasn't very relevant to a SEC, was it? Nonetheless, as I said, kindness is important. If nothing else, it makes you likeable, and likeability is one of the biggest requirements for a SEC.

13 LIKEABLE

Likeable (*adjective*):
Pleasant, someone who is liked (or capable of being liked) by others –
I'd say popular, but that wouldn't be entirely accurate – it's more like a
sequence – if you're likeable, people will like you, and if people like you,
you'd be popular.
Example: That boy is so polite and pleasant, no wonder he is well-liked.

***

You can't be a SEC if people – especially the older generation – don't
like you. You also have to be reasonably popular with your peer group – if
you're some asocial, taciturn creature hiding in a corner, even if you are the
smartest or most talented person in the room, you're going to get nowhere,
and you're definitely not going to be an exemplary character of legends.
Not that I'm saying that people want to be a SEC. Some do, some don't
– it takes all sorts.
Anyhow – the point is, it is good to be likeable, even if you don't intend
to be a SEC. And if you do intend to be a SEC, you *must* be likeable. It's
not that difficult – you just need to be nice in general. There's no need to
be a saint or anything. Just help out people around you, and be nice about
it. (I know of people who are very kind but not nice at all – they're not
likeable people. On the other hand, I also know of very likeable people who
are not kind at all. Some are not even nice people – they just pretend to be
pleasant.)
That's the key – being pleasant. Make people enjoy your company. It's a
basic business skill, too – no one's going to want to deal with you (which is
bad for business) if they can't stand your presence.
Of course, you also need to guard against being too nice. That's a big

no-no, and an invitation to people to step all over you. Not good at all. Everything in moderation – including likeability. People who are too likeable are trouble magnets. Believe me, I know. I grew up with two of them.

Both Big Brother and Little Sister are very attractive, as I've mentioned previously. Big Brother tends to push people away by exaggerating his eccentricity, while Little Sister likes to convert people into her devotees to do her bidding. Both are scary in their own way.

Big Brother's actions are a side-effect from his time in college, when someone actually broke his heart. Women and men flock to him like bees – his appeal transcends gender. And then they start flirting with him and he feels cornered. And then he uses his incredible mind to alienate them as much (and as fast) as he possibly can.

The scene usually runs like this:

Big Brother appears (probably dripping pheromones that the family has become immune to) in public. At least forty percent of the public migrates to his side – batting eyelashes, throwing out innuendos, making flirty comments, showing off to capture his attention – it's almost like a mating dance ritual. Big Brother is, after all, a dashing combination of the looks of a superstar with the softness of an intellectual and the nobility of a gentleman.

There was this one time when a very influential person (of our parents' age group) approached Big Brother at a post-conference dinner, put a hand on his arm and said, "My handsome boy, I'd be glad to fund your next research project. If you'd like to talk about it, I'm in Room #308."

The innocent brainiac that he is, Big Brother didn't even understand what that meant. Fortunately, we have appointed half a dozen assistants for him, with the mandate that at no point must he be left alone when he's outside (unless he's with Mum, Dad, Little Sister or me), and there should be at least two or three of them around him at all times. Three of his assistants are reformed hitmen pretending to be slow but diligent researchers. (Big Brother doesn't know. Little Sister found them and converted them into her lackeys when we encountered them – but that's a story for another time.)

One of the assistants quickly whispered in Big Brother's ear, explaining what that meant.

Big Brother promptly turned green and proceeded to vomit all over this person's clothes. No one except Little Sister believes me when I say this – but I'm convinced that Big Brother can calculate the exact initial angle required for the optimum trajectory for his vomit's projectile motion to deliver maximum damage to the intended subject. He's done this too many times for it to be coincidence.

Yes, Big Brother's favourite method of dealing with people who try to harass him is to throw up on them. I bet he's set up some sort of record for barfing on the highest number of people or something. I can think of at least thirty such people off the top of my head. There are probably many more.

Anyway – the point here is that being too likeable is also rather troublesome. So people who are naturally attractive need to be more careful when working on their likeability quotient. It's easy to mess up.

As for Little Sister – she can inflict more damage with two fingers than an army tank. And she can inflict more damage with her tongue than an army of lawyers. With a face of an angel and the charm of a demon, she can decimate *anyone* who dares to annoy her. She has four assistants, and each one of these individuals is more skilled than a field agent. Well, it's not surprising – they all trained with her. Also, Little Sister is a bit mysophobic – so the quartet (that's what Big Brother and I call her assistants) don't even let anyone breathe on her, let alone touch her. Despite this, people flock to her. Well, she does have the face and voice of an angel. She often looks like she's either walked out of a painting or off a fashion show ramp.

Compared to these two, I'm blessedly ordinary. I'm moderately handsome and moderately pleasant – and most definitely *not* a trouble magnet. I'm just the right amount of likeable – people think I'm nice, but not enough to flock around me mindlessly or to lure me in. So I have a normal social life.

14 METICULOUS

Meticulous (*adjective*):
Careful, precise, detail-oriented.
Example: She is so meticulous that her account books are accurate to three decimal points.

***

A meticulous person is always well received – not only as a SEC, but also when you grow up and start working. Being careful and precise and paying attention to details is good. Useful in pretty much every walk of life.

This is especially true for me since I run a business. Fortunately for me, I was raised to be meticulous from a fairly young age – from the age of five, to be precise. (No one cared at the orphanage – but Mum and Dad are very particular about these things. Also, Big Brother being the super-brainy type, it's easiest to communicate with him in precise terms. If you ask him vague questions, he's at a loss. He's very meticulous himself, and since I idolised him, I tried to do everything he did. I was quite a copycat in the initial days until I grew comfortable in my own skin…that, too, is something I owe to my Big Brother.)

Of course, one needs to be a little tolerant here as well and not to take it to the extreme. (Which Dad and Big Brother are sometimes wont to do.) There was this time Mum and I had gone shopping for clothes for everyone for a family gathering – it was a themed party. Little Sister had decided that we were going to attend as the Addams family, so Mum and I were taking care of the costumes, and Little Sister was in charge of the make-up. Dad and Big Brother were supposed to just turn up, because both of them were really busy with some project at the time.

Now, it's not always possible to get exact costumes like TV characters, right? Mum and I got the best approximations that we could, and Little Sister said she'd figure out the make-up accordingly.

When we were taking the measurements for preparing the costumes, however, Big Brother went ballistic because he said the characters we'd settled on were wrong. Mum and Dad would be Patricia and Gomez, that was fine. We'd thought between Big Brother and I, one could be Uncle Fester and one could be Lurch, and Littler Sister would be Wednesday. Big Brother, however, said the family would never go out for a gathering without Pugsley, So I offered to be Pugsley. But Big Brother rejected that and insisted that I had to be Wednesday and Little Sister would be Pugsley, because Pugsley was younger. Neither Little Sister nor I were happy with that.

Ultimately, we went as the Justice League. Fortunately, there were many characters to choose from, so we didn't have much conflict – although, Big Brother was a little unhappy about the colour of his mask because it wasn't exactly the same shade as the Martian Manhunter and Dad wasn't too thrilled about his makeshift Batmobile, either. Mum, Little Sister and I had a lot of fun, though.

15 NEUTRAL

Neutral (*adjective*):
Impartial, not supporting either side in a conflict.
Example: Country X is taking a neutral position by not taking either party's side in the dispute between Country Y and Country Z.

***

It might sound odd that this is relevant for a SEC, but it is. While it is natural to have one's personal biases, it is best for a SEC to remain neutral in case of conflicts. Why? Because only a neutral party can resolve a conflict appropriately. And resolving conflicts is a delicate balance – you risk the chance of offending everyone, especially if these are people dear to you. Sometimes, you know you feel too strongly about it or you care too much about one of the parties to be able to act neutrally and won't be able to keep your personal feelings out of it – in those cases, it's best to respectfully decline the mediator or judge's role.

For example, if a conflict involves Mum, Dad, Big Brother or Little Sister, I know I'm unconditionally biased in their favour – so while I can negotiate on their behalf or attempt to resolve it on their behalf – I can never be a neutral mediator or observer or adjudicator. And that wouldn't be fair to the other party.

But barring such things, it's best to keep a cool head and think of things from an impartial point of view – to see both sides of the conflict. That's the key to dispute resolution. And let me tell you – as the President and Vice-President of the Student Association in B-school, Bestie and I were often called upon to settle disputes. So being neutral kind of became our default state of existence. We became almost immune to drama and hysteria by the time our term ended. (We stayed out of the next election – one needs to enjoy their college life, too.)

Sometimes we were called in for inane issues, and sometimes things were rather bizarre. A lot of problems involved romantic entanglements. Once, we were called in to deal with a fighting couple – he said that she was cheating on him with another guy, and she said he was cheating on her with another guy as well – this "another guy" for both him and her being the same person. As it turned out – the guy and the girl both had fallen in love with this "another guy" – and this third person was a rather villainous (but enchanting) character, who teased and flirted with half the people on campus (regardless of gender, and sometimes even age or marital/commitment status) – and he was just playing around with these two. Neither of them had really cheated on the other…but they broke up afterwards anyway – I mean, if you're not attracted to your significant other and you don't trust them either, there's no point in continuing the relationship, right?

16 OBSERVANT

Observant (*adjective*):
Quick to notice things.
Example: She observed the clenching of his fists and moved away before he could hit her.

***

Oh, this is a good one, and ties in with a lot of others. You notice a lot of subtle things if you're observant, and it helps you determine your own actions accordingly.

For example, if Little Sister is rubbing her eyes when she turns up for breakfast, she's tired and needs a cup of coffee instead of her usual green tea. If Mum's drumming her fingers on the armrest, she's stressed and needs something sweet, preferably chocolate dipped almonds. If Dad's tapping his chin, he's irritated and needs something cold to drink to cool him down – guiness or pineapple juice work best in these times, depending on where he is. If Big Brother is stroking the bridge of his nose, he's had a brilliant idea and it's best to slide some writing instruments under his nose (or he'll start writing on whatever he sees with whatever is at hand...once he wrote stuff with ketchup on his soup plate and threw a fit when soup was served – the maid was new, she didn't know about his idiosyncrasies at the time).

The power of observation enhances a lot of other parameters – courtesy, geniality, likeability and so on. You don't need to be Sherlock Holmes – you just need to pay a little attention to people and things. And sometimes, you need to bring things to other people's attention – because even though you may observe something, you may not know its significance. Anomalies are important.

Like the time at the club when we nearly got crushed to death – well, that might be an exaggeration, but we could have ended up with serious injury. This was a club Mum and Dad frequented, and we'd been there plenty of times. Their food is excellent. We even have a favourite table. It's by the window and overlooks the garden, and there's an antique chandelier right above it.

Our family of five was seated at our favourite table, waiting for the first course to arrive. I was admiring the chandelier (yet again – I love beautiful things) and suddenly noticed a small crack on the ceiling. There was live music on the stage that day, and a few minutes later, I realised that the crack had gotten slightly bigger.

Curious, I pointed it out to Big Brother. He looked at the crack, then looked at the singer, and then looked at his watch. His face contorted with horror.

"Sis, get Mum away!" he shouted, simultaneously grabbing Dad and I and dragging us away from the table.

Little Sister has lightning fast reflexes, so she and Mum were already halfway across the room.

"Big Brother, what are you doing?" I asked, unsettled. He rarely acted this way…but he had been under a lot of pressure lately.

Before he could reply, the singer hit a high note, the chandelier shook and then fell upon the table with an almighty crash.

Dad, Big Brother and I were scratched a little by some flying shrapnel, but nothing major. Thanks to Little Sister's extraordinary reflexes, she and Mum were completely unscathed.

The club's management couldn't apologise enough. We didn't plan to sue them or anything – it was an accident, after all. It could have been a tragedy, but thanks to Big Brother's amazing brain, we were saved. But that amazing brain wouldn't have figured out the outcome without my small observation, you see?

17 PERSEVERANCE

Perseverance (*noun*):

Not giving up – continuing your efforts even if there's no success or results visible.

Example: She persevered for several months before she finally started to lose weight.

***

As they say – if at first you don't succeed, try, try and try until you do. No one is born perfect, and no one gets anywhere without learning things and working on them. Even demi-gods like Big Brother and Little Sister – they, too, work for their success. They, too, fail sometimes. But they don't give up. They keep at it until they get it. And if even these two extraordinary creatures need to persevere to achieve something, we mere mortals need to persevere even more.

Grades, for example. You have to keep working at it if you want to maintain good grades or get better grades. Same with competitions. I persevered for nearly two years before I was able to last more than five minutes in a fencing match with my teacher. But when I finally did, it felt amazing. In fact, the longer the perseverance, the more the diligence, the greater the sense of achievement when you are finally able to accomplish success. If you give up halfway, you're definitely not going anywhere.

I do realise that it can be very difficult to keep yourself motivated as you try to keep going when things aren't working out. The constant string of failure tends to chip away at the strongest of spirits. It's not easy to pick yourself up every time you fall. But you can always reach out to your loved ones for moral support. I do.

Like the fencing practice I just spoke of. I got interested in fencing because I saw it in a movie and found it absolutely fascinating. Mum and Dad have always been the type to encourage us to learn new things, so when I told them that I wanted to learn fencing, they promptly arranged for a teacher for me. So, thrice a week I would be driven down to the teacher's studio to learn and practise with other kids. Some had been learning for a while. Some were good, some were average and some were bad. Initially, I was the worst one in the class. I couldn't even hold the blade properly, let alone swing it.

But I practised. Not just at the studio; at home as well. I'd sneak out of my bedroom in the middle of the night, go to the garden (trust me, you don't want to swing a blade around indoors, especially when you can't control the blade yet) and I would practise for at least an hour or two.

A few months later, however, I hadn't made much progress at all. It was very frustrating. It was the first time in my short life so far that I was really, truly bad at something I wanted to learn. I was miserable. One day, after another abysmal practice session at the studio, I came home and told my parents that I didn't want to learn fencing anymore.

They were surprised, because I had clearly been very enthusiastic about it earlier.

"I thought you really liked fencing," Mum said. "You've been working hard."

"We know you practise in the middle of the night," Dad remarked. "Clearly you're quite devoted to it. So why do you want to quit?"

"Because I'm really bad at it," I said glumly. "It's been months, but I'm awful. I'm the third last in the practice group at the studio."

"Ah, so it's your first taste of not being good at something," Mum observed. "That can be difficult."

"But that's still not a reason to give up," Dad said. "Why did you want to learn fencing in the first place, Seccy?"

"Because I thought it was cool," I confessed.

"And do you still think it's cool?" he asked.

I nodded.

"And you want to be cool?" he continued.

I nodded again.

"Then just keep at it. Even if it takes you longer than usual to learn. As long as you don't give up, you will learn," he concluded.

"But if you give up, it'll never get better," Mum added. "If you want to achieve something, you must persevere until you reach your goal. If you quit in the middle, you'll never reach."

"Think of it as a long journey – like when we go to visit someone," Dad explained. "If you want to visit this person, you have to complete the journey, right? If halfway on the road you say that it's too hot and you don't want to go further because you got tired of the heat, you're never going to end up visiting, right? You have to finish your journey."

"And learning is exactly like that," Mum said. "Did I ever tell you how long it was before I could play a simple tune on the violin instead of producing ear-splitting screeches?"

I shook my head.

"Five years," she said proudly. "I've got no musical talent, but I really, really wanted to play the violin. So I kept going until I could."

I was quite impressed, and pleased that Mum told me about her experience. This was very encouraging. If even someone as amazing as Mum had faced trouble while learning something and could only overcome the hurdle by persevering, I decided I could do so, too.

And I did.

And finally, one day, several years later, I managed to disarm my teacher in a perfectly executed move. That day, I couldn't stop smiling. Actually, I couldn't stop smiling the entire week. It felt so good, so much better than something easily achievable. Oh boy, I can still feel the giddiness when I think about it.

18 QUIRKY

Quirky (*adjective*):
Peculiar, strange.
Example: She has a habit of drinking a glass of pineapple juice every time she has a meeting with the Chairman – otherwise she wouldn't touch pineapples with a five-foot pole.

***

Cute little quirks make one quaint – and are often the signature of a SEC. More brownie points if these are productive quirks. Like Little Sister's habit of labelling everything. She even labels her label makers. It's cute and funny and downright useful when you need something. Yes, there's a printed index. We all use it on the sly.

Mum and Dad are obsessed with symmetry and the number five. There's a five-year age gap between them, and each of us siblings. All three of us were adopted at the age of five. The difference between each of our ages and our parents' ages are multiples of five. Every building we own (be it residential or commercial) has rooms in multiples of five.

Big Brother has a habit of separating his food by colour, and he eats them in the order of darkest to lightest. Yes, he'll eat the chocolate truffle first and the white radish last. And he hates it if colours are mixed up on his plate. Hmm…maybe that's why he's always ready to puke on annoying people especially at lunch or dinner gatherings.

As for me – I have a little quirk that made me really popular in school. It's more a whimsical memory trick than a quirk – but well, it's strange and peculiar, so it probably qualifies as a quirk, too. When I need to mug up boring things (for exams, for work, for any reason), I make up stories to help me remember these things. And they're often quite funny – well, I like funny things.

For example, when we had to learn those long, complicated chemical formulae of all sorts of compounds in school, I used to weave fairy tales around them. The lattice would become the winding path the hero needed to take to reach his destination. The first element would be the main character, and the last would be the love interest waiting to be rescued. At each point, there would be an adventure/task to be completed or an opponent to face. I used to keep flashcards with a portrait, a backstory and defined personality traits for each element on the periodic table. (I wonder where the deck is now. I'll ask Mum if I can't find it in Little Sister's index.) I remember Gold was a flashy, snobbish blonde guy with amber eyes who started and ended each sentence he spoke with "Au!" – so, he'd say, "Au! Seccy, how can you forget that I don't mix with the commoners, Au? Au! Why do you think I'd react with that lowly element, Au?" Hydrogen was a hyperactive, bouncy little kid with borderline pyromania. Carbon was a dark-haired gloomy character that appeared uninvited everywhere and was super clingy. Sodium was a good-looking guy in drag. Mercury was a domineering lady.

Ah, that makes me nostalgic.

19 RESPONSIBLE

Responsible (*adjective*):
Dutiful, trustworthy – someone who fulfils their duty, or keeps their word, and/or acts prudently.
Example: He is a responsible citizen; he never drinks and drives.

***

Responsibility is a highly desirable quality for any person – regardless of whether they are a SEC or not. Everyone likes a responsible person.

I might have mentioned before, some of the qualities exhibited by a SEC are actually leadership qualities/skills. Responsibility is one of them. Responsibility is not just one thing. It comprises of many things – doing what you're supposed to do (and not doing what you're not supposed to do), following the rules, fulfilling your duty, keeping your promises, taking charge…there's a long list.

As a great man once told Spiderman – "With great power comes great responsibility."

Then there are different types of responsibilities. One person plays many roles in society – there are personal relationships and professional relationships. Every relationship comes with its own responsibilities.

For example, as a class monitor, it is my duty to ensure that everyone in my class follows the school rules and if they don't, I have to report it to the teacher.

As a student, my responsibility would be to study sincerely and do the best I can at the exams.

Similarly, as the Managing Director of a company, it is my responsibility to ensure that my business is up and running, my employees have the resources they need and that they are utilising these resources appropriately to perform their assigned tasks. It is also my responsibility to supervise the things they do and to pay their salaries.

As a friend, part of my responsibility is to ensure that my friends don't get into trouble, and if they do get into trouble, it is my responsibility to help them fix it.

As a brother, it is my responsibility to love and support my siblings. As a son, it is my responsibility to listen to and look after my parents (not that they need looking after, but still).

As a lover (for when I do finally date someone), it would be responsibility to love and cherish the person I'm dating and not cheat on them.

Everyone has responsibilities in different aspects of their lives. It is good to think about it and make oneself aware of one's responsibility. Only when you know what you need to do will you do it.

20 STUDIOUS

Studious (*adjective*):
Someone who studies a lot.
Example: He is a studious child; no wonder he gets top grades.

***

This one is a no-brainer, right? The primary purpose of a SEC is to motivate kids to study more. If the SEC being held up as an example is not a studious kid, how would the comparison be effective?

I have said before that I have a high IQ. But having a high IQ doesn't mean I don't need to study or learn. It just means that I learn faster than others. But I still have to study. IQ is just the raw material, and studying is like the process of developing the finished product. It's like having a fine piece of silk fabric – unless that fabric is stitched into an outfit, it's going to be useless, right?

And that's why, to learn things and to maintain my grades, I needed to study. And I studied a lot. I liked studying. I spent a lot of my free time in the library, learning new things. I was (and still am) a bookworm. I read and I read and I read. I probably read the most in my family. Good thing my parents have a lot of books at home – and even better that they're rich. Otherwise, I might have bankrupted them with my propensity to buy books. I still read a lot.

When I was a kid, I used to carry books with me everywhere (even to parties and sleepovers, and even when I knew that there would not be any chance to read them) – in fact, I still do that. Habit of a lifetime. Well, these days it's one physical book and an e-book reader with tons of books, but still. Why the physical book? Because I love the smell of paper.

So, whenever I was seen in public, it was with a book in hand. Now, a child carrying books around all the time looks like an angel to most people – especially if they have kids. So, obviously, I became a SEC.

Initially, I used to study a lot because I wanted to be like Big Brother. I studied very hard to catch up to him – that continued throughout my school life. Even though I never managed to catch up with him, I did enjoy the process very much.

Plus, Big Brother is a benevolent creature. And he loves me – well, sometimes I think he loves Little Sister more than he loves me from the way he dotes on her…but then, she *is* the baby of the family and *everybody* dotes on her. Even I do.

Right, so going back to the point. Big Brother is a benevolent creature, and he likes to dispense knowledge. I think he was as excited as I was when I got adopted, because he'd sit with me every day and help me with my homework, and he'd also teach me new things. Even though I was much slower than him, he didn't mind teaching me. Maybe he enjoyed teaching me as much I enjoyed learning from him. (Also, other than himself, I was the smartest kid Big Brother knew until Little Sister was adopted.) Those are some of my fondest memories.

21 TOLERANT

Tolerant (*adjective*):
Someone who respects others' views and/or endures patiently.
Example: He is very tolerant of the mess his naughty cat creates.

***

Getting along with people is an important quality for a SEC, and you need to be tolerant to be able to deal with all kinds of people. Not everyone is nice or pleasant, but you still need to associate with them, so you need to endure patiently.

However, this is also one of the things that needs to be practised in moderation. Being too tolerant would make you a doormat and then everyone will walk all over you and you'd be pathetic, right? So you need to be cautious, and you have to draw the line somewhere.

But generally, it is good to be tolerant…until the line is breached.

We used to have an employee – he was a brilliant fellow and exceptional at his work. I had recruited him myself, and I was very happy with his performance in general. He was very talented, and I enjoyed exchanging ideas or discussing new issues with him. He was well-read and well-spoken, and generally seemed to have a good temperament. I liked him very much.

However, a few months later, I suddenly started receiving complaints from his female colleagues. I believe in an open-door policy, and I've always encouraged my employees to come directly and speak to me.

When I was suddenly flooded with complaints about this guy, I was shocked to the core. His performance was still exceptional – however, his personality seemed to have undergone a drastic change. He was increasingly rude to his female colleagues – to the point that he left some of them in tears. The work environment was rapidly becoming toxic and I didn't want to happen at all. After all, if my employees are not happy, they wouldn't be able to work optimally – and that'd be bad for the business.

So I asked HR to look into the guy, and while they were conducting their investigation, I pulled him away and put him on an exclusive project to work directly with me, limiting his interactions with everyone else. We worked seamlessly and harmoniously for a few days – and my female employees were quite relieved that they didn't have to put up with him every day.

Then the HR report appeared on my table. I read it quickly and realised that the man's wife had left him recently and run away with a much younger guy – and as if that was not bad enough, she'd taken all the portable valuables and liquid cash she could lay her hands on. It was a tragic situation and I sympathised with him, but I couldn't tolerate his toxic behaviour with my female employees.

So I discussed the matter with him frankly. He broke down completely and I ended up taking him to a psychiatrist. After a few months of therapy, he was a new man, and his work performance was even better than before. When he returned, he apologised properly to his female colleagues – they were quite forgiving because I'd told them about the situation beforehand.

This guy now heads one of the associate companies, and he's made it one of the most profitable ones under our banner. Isn't that great?

22 UBIQUITOUS

Ubiquitous (*adjective*):
Appearing or found everywhere.
Example: You seem to appear everywhere these days.

***

Well, not literally, but visibility is important for a SEC. If people don't see you, how will they know about you and your achievement? It mustn't be an occasional glance, either. You need to make your presence felt and your absence matter. You need to make strategic appearances at frequent intervals. You know the old adage – out of sight, out of mind. That's what happens to a SEC who sits quietly in a corner and studies – soon enough, they're forgotten, and once they're forgotten, they're no longer a SEC. How can you give an example of someone you don't even remember?

So that's why it is important to stay visible and stay relevant. Be fresh in everyone's memory as much as possible. People should say, "Oh, Seccy, I seem to see you everywhere." Or "Oh, Seccy, I hear of you everywhere these days."

There is no moderation in this – well, except that your appearances shouldn't be annoying. It'd better be like a breath of fresh air. Media can also be employed – after all, digital presence is all-encompassing.

Speaking of which, Bestie is a digital wizard – he revamped all our websites, and the finished products were just outstanding. A lot of my visibility is thanks to him.

The first time I asked him to help me with this, we were still in school, and I'd just been given my company. I knew how good Bestie was at this stuff, so naturally I wanted to rope him in.

He was a bit unsure, though. "Seccy, I'm not as clever as you," he told me.

"Nonsense," I replied. "You can do a hell lot of things I can't. This digital stuff is just one of them."

He smiled slightly. "Yes, but…"

I held up a hand to stop him. "Tell me this first – are you capable of doing this or not?"

He hesitated for a moment. Then he said softly, "Yes, I think I can."

"Then that's good enough for me. Why isn't it good enough for you? I believe in my Bestie. You should, too!" I nagged.

He burst out laughing. "Can't win with you, can I?" he mumbled. "All right, then, I'll do it for you."

We high-fived. And that's how our first website was made. Of course, it didn't have my picture or my name, because I worked behind-the-scenes for a few years, but Bestie did such an amazing job that Mum and Dad went gaga over it.

So, naturally, we roped him in to revamp the entire group's digital content.

Once we were done with B-school, Bestie set up his own firm. He has the exclusive contract for our entire group…in fact, most of his clients have an exclusive contract with him – he's that good, really.

So, nowadays, if you see me or hear of me everywhere in a non-annoying way, you can bet that it's my best friend's job.

23 VERSATILE

Versatile (*adjective*):
Able to do many different things – kind of like a jack-of-all-trades.
Example: He knows about stock markets as well as cooking – isn't he a versatile fellow?

***

Functional human beings need to be multi-faceted these days – and it's doubly so for a SEC. Never underestimate the power of versatility! It's not like you have to everything – but being able to do a wide range of things is definitely an asset.

Mum and Dad have always laid great emphasis on this. Even Big Brother with his negligible life-skills is quite versatile. Little Sister and I are much better than him, though.

It has to be viable versatility, though – which is why I'm the SEC, since I'm closest to the proverbial jack-of-all-trades. Big Brother and Little Sister are pretty much masters of everything they do.

Big Brother often says that I'm too modest and underestimate myself, but I don't think that's the case. I think I'm fairly factual and realistic. I know my strengths and weaknesses and I act accordingly. I know there are things only I can do in the family. And I know that there are things I can't. Logical analysis is one of my top skills.

So, back to versatility – it's also fun to involve yourself in different kinds of things, you know? Life can get boring – and boring people do not last long as a SEC – and it's good to mix things up a bit and keep it interesting.

When I was a kid, I got praised for both my academic performance and my extra-curricular activities by people. (Remember, I was the one with the "achievable" status.) I often dragged my friends into these activities as well – it's no fun being a SEC by myself. Between the six of us, we usually won about two-thirds of all things up for grabs.

Once, I even managed to win a prize in every category (half of them were consolation prizes, but still) – I was in the fifth grade, and Little Sister was going to join us soon (we all went to the same school), and I wanted her to see how cool I was, too. (Big Brother was already cool, plus he hardly cares about these things. Also, he was going away to college soon. He'd outgrown even the advanced classes by then.)

So, for once, I registered myself for all the competition categories being held for our annual day. I already had the academic achievement prize in my basket. While I won the first prize in only one of the categories, I bagged a second prize and a couple of third prizes as well. The rest were consolation prizes.

When I went up on stage for the fourth time, the chief guest joked that he might as well give me a chair to sit on stage and save me the effort of coming up and going down each time. The headmistress laughed and said that was not a bad idea.

Of course, that ended up drawing even more attention to me. Whispers of "Oh, what a good child", "Learn from him", "I wish my kid was like this" and so on broke out in the hall. I returned to my seat between Mum and Dad, both of whom were beaming proudly at me. Big Brother patted my shoulder, and Little Sister looked at me with shining eyes full of admiration. My friends, who knew that I'd been working hard to impress the new Little Sister, began to narrate embellished tales of my greatness until I nearly died of embarrassment.

But then, Little Sister said, "Brother Seccy is so cool! I want to be like you!"

And I was over the moon.

24 WORTHY

Worthy (*adjective*):
Deserving affection, attention, effort, praise, respect etc.
Example: The seven-course meal she prepared by herself made her worthy of being called a master chef.

***

Now, unless you're deemed worthy of being a SEC, how could you be a SEC? This worth could be of various types – highlighting the exemplary qualities a SEC possesses – but it's not self-worth we're talking about here; this is a classic case of "beauty lies in the eyes of the beholder".

Like that time Big Brother dressed up as a vampire for a costume party he was forced to attend (Little Sister threw it, so he didn't really have a choice – sometimes I'm quite jealous of how easily Little Sister can get anyone in the family to do things she wants, while I have to argue like a prized lawyer and convince them rationally – or beseech them on my knees when all else fails!) – thinking that he looked scary and everyone would naturally avoid him. My poor, dear Big Brother didn't realise that the outfit made him look even more attractive – with all the bad boy appeal – and the party ended with Little Sister and I *literally* throwing people off him. It was hilarious. For several weeks after that, he'd throw a book at us (his aim is scarily accurate, he probably calculates the angles and everything in his head before he throws anything) if we even mentioned the word "vampire". Little Sister with her lightning fast reflexes usually dodged or used me as a human shield, so I was the one that ended up bruised and battered. A friend even enquired if I had developed a sudden interest in extreme sports.

Then there was the time a similar thing happened to Little Sister (and it got a little troublesome). We were visiting Granny and Gramps, and

Gramps was being given some fancy award by the university for his great contribution to education and all. Granny decided it would be a good idea to have Little Sister play the piano at the award function. Superb idea, for Little Sister is extremely talented. The only glitch was that when Little Sister asked what she should play, Granny said, "Something that would make your Gramps happy."

Now, Gramps doesn't really like classical music. What he likes is rock n roll.

So our clever Little Sister composed a piano score blending rock n roll – overnight. She didn't really think it was a work of genius; she merely thought of it as a fun piece she wrote for Gramps to enjoy.

It would still have been ok – everyone would have praised her music, been awed by her slender fingers flying over the piano keys, and we'd be done with it…but as luck would have it, one of the attendees was a Hollywood music director who knew his stuff – he was Granny's classmate from her London days. This guy naturally realised what a prodigious talent Little Sister was, and made her a very public offer of a ridiculously high sum to come and work with him for his next movie music. That was still ok, because if Little Sister was interested in the project, we'd fully support her. What was unfortunate was that some of her former relatives – the ones who couldn't wait to get rid of her when she was a small child who'd just lost her parents in a tragic accident – happened to witness this, and were suddenly all over her, wanting a share of the pie and shamelessly claiming her to be their favourite, poor, orphaned niece. The Hollywood guy looked a little shocked, because he knew Little Sister to be Granny's granddaughter.

Little Sister reacted beautifully. With a cold face, she turned to our parents and asked, "Mum, Dad, are you related to these people?"

"Not at all, dearie," Mum said cheerfully.

"Then why are they bothering me?" Little Sister asked innocently. That angelic face really comes in handy sometimes.

"Because they want to ride your coattails," Big Brother replied.

"I'm afraid my coattails can't bear so much dead weight," Little Sister said sweetly to the shameless bunch of people. "Please stay away from me."

"You ungrateful child!" someone shouted. "Did you forget that we took care of you when you were nothing but a small orphan?"

Dad stepped forward menacingly. "Need I remind you of the quality of your care?" he asked dangerously.

I stepped up next to him. It would be a metaphorical bloodbath if Dad really lost his temper. Not that I didn't understand his rage; I was quite angry, too.

"We are happy to discuss this either legally or socially at a more appropriate time and place," I said politely, handing out my business card.

"Please get in touch with me at your convenience."

What I'd handed out was my figurative heir-to-the-throne card. I didn't really like pulling rank or intimidating people like this, but I could be very ruthless when someone threatened my family.

I spotted Little Sister smirking at me. She mouthed "cool" at me, and I felt the dark anger creeping up on me settle a bit.

The pack of wannabe parasites shot Dad and I a terrified look and backed off. I knew I'd have to do some damage control for the wagging tongues later – but that wasn't a big deal.

The Hollywood guy looked rather awkward. "I'm sorry," he said sincerely to Little Sister. "I got too excited; I should have waited to speak privately with you. I do hope you would consider the offer, though."

I could see that she was tempted. Sure enough, she turned to Mum and Dad. "May I?" she asked.

"Of course, dearie," Mum said.

"Go out and have fun," Dad told her. "It's fortunate that you get to learn from someone so accomplished."

So Little Sister went off to Hollywood for a few months.

All's well that ends well, I suppose.

Right – so the moral of the story is – self-worth doesn't matter sometimes; public opinion does. You may think you're doing something perfectly ordinary, but it may be considered an incredible achievement by other people. Or vice versa.

25 XANY

Xany (*adjective*):
Having a lot of energy – maybe a little wild.
Example: Her sixth salsa dance in a row – how xany!

***

This is pretty much self-explanatory, isn't it? How can you be a SEC if you have no energy? You don't need to be as xany as…say, the Energizer Bunny, but you do need to have enough energy to finish everything that you're supposed to (or that you said you would) and still not look utterly exhausted – in public, at least. The frail, fatigued look doesn't work well for a SEC.

I know this first-hand. There was this time when I fell ill in class, and my SEC status took a nosedive for quite some time, since a lot of people thought I'd overworked myself into illness. Which wasn't true at all, but the truth didn't matter. No one's going to want to have their own kids emulate someone who gets sick easily, especially if it seems like the sickness was caused by themselves.

Well, I suppose I am to blame for what happened more or less. Although it wasn't overwork.

Mum and Dad were away on a business trip for a few days. Big Brother was at some research lab in a remote corner of the world. Little Sister was away on a school camping trip. I was by myself for a few days. I wasn't bored or anything – I was a member of a couple of student committees and the school annual day was coming up, so I was fairly busy myself.

Which is why I ignored the mild abdominal pain – it wasn't a major inconvenience, and it didn't hurt all that much. Besides, if I mentioned it to the housekeeper, she'd tell my parents, and one of them would immediately fly home. I didn't want to disrupt their schedule. Besides, I thought I'd overeaten or something, and it'd go away on its own.

I was wrong. By the third day, the magnitude of my discomfort had increased significantly. Since Mum and Dad were returning in a couple of days, I thought it'd be ok to ignore it a little longer.

On the fourth day, I collapsed in class, scaring the living daylights out of my friends. I was rushed to the hospital, and when I woke up a few hours later, my family was poring over me anxiously, and I learnt that my inflamed appendix had been removed.

"Why are you here?" I asked my family, even though I knew the answer to that. I'd expected one of them to fly back immediately – not all four!

"What do you mean, why are we here?" Big Brother snapped. "You suddenly collapsed and no one knew anything! You little idiot – why didn't you tell someone if you were in pain and get it checked?"

"Er…it wasn't really that bad…" I mumbled. "I thought I ate something that didn't agree with me."

"You expect us to believe that?" Little Sister said angrily. "Did you donate all your IQ points while we weren't looking? Don't you know the symptoms of appendicitis?!"

I did, actually, but I didn't connect the dots until right before I collapsed. As it turned out, since I'd not spoken to anyone about feeling any discomfort, no one knew why I'd collapsed, making everyone panic – especially since I'm usually healthy as a horse. A lot of time was wasted in running unnecessary tests (the hospital belonged to Mum and Dad, after all, and Mum was the Chairperson, so they wouldn't risk misdiagnosing one of their kids, not to mention I knew most of the doctors and the staff here, and was even well-liked). If I'd spoken up earlier about my abdominal pain, it would have been much simpler.

Ouch. I'd messed up. I looked up guiltily at the red-rimmed eyes of my parents and siblings.

Mum patted my arm. "Seccy, you know it's not ok to let any illness fester untreated, don't you? Did you forget your parents are also doctors?"

I shook my head. "I'm sorry. I honestly did think it was something I ate," I told her. "It was very mild and escalated suddenly. I didn't want to bother you when you were away for work over a minor thing."

Dad rubbed his face tiredly. "Don't you know by now that *nothing* is more important to us than our children?"

"I'm sorry," I repeated.

But looking at my family like this…them abandoning everything and rushing to my side…I couldn't help but feel warm and happy.

I tend act a little spoilt and selfish when I'm ill, and I like it when they dote on me. So, for the next few days, I gave in to my urge and did exactly that. Mum, Dad, Big Brother and Little Sister indulged me as if I was a spoilt little prince. Even my friends and classmates who turned up with flowers and cards were roped into the act. For a few days, I pretended to be either a precious, fragile beauty or the supreme ruler of my world – depending on my mood. It was quite enjoyable for me, and everyone else also looked like they were having fun pampering me.

Then it passed and I was back to my xany self soon enough.

26 YOUTHFUL

Youthful (*adjective*):
    Young, full of youth.
    Example: Such an innocent, youthful worldview…

***

Adults can't be a SEC – it's specifically meant for the younger generation, as long as their parents/guardians have some say in their upbringing and/or affairs. Which is why it is important for a SEC to be either actually young – a child is the best – or at least someone youthful enough to not be a full blown "grown-up".

Why? Well, the older you grow, the more resistant to change you are. Also, other people's opinions matter less and less as you grow older. (Probably why really old people are the most whimsical of all.) Kids, however, crave their parents'/guardians'/teachers' approval, so that's where a SEC is used most often. As long as one craves childish recognition from someone is a superior position, a SEC is useful.

Technically, it could be used in professional situations as well, but I doubt it'd have much effect. Employees do care about what their bosses think of them, but comparing them to other people…I'm not saying it doesn't happen, because it does – I'm just not sure how effective it is. Generally, people don't like to be compared to others, especially when they're the ones falling short. It'd only make the workplace rather tense and unhappy – but that's just my thought. Kids, that way, are far more broad-minded than adults, and simpler in their desires. All they want is to be praised by their parents/guardians/teachers, and if learning a skill or achieving something similar to another peer is going to get them that coveted appreciation, they'll just go ahead and do it.

Hence the use of "child" in SEC and not an ambiguous "human". Also, there's the element of care. Parents do a lot of unpleasant things because it is ultimately for the benefit of their child – and using a SEC is one of these. The idea is to motivate their own kids and help them achieve success – there's no malice or bad intent behind these comparisons. It's not that they love their own child less; it's the other way round. It's because they love their child that they use a SEC. They don't want to go and adopt the SEC they're talking about. They don't particularly care about the SEC himself/herself – they only care that using a SEC in their speech could help their own kid. Parents are pretty focused that way.

And of course, the element of youth is helpful here. It is easy to hold up someone young as an example to another young person. A peer or an older person would be comparable to oneself – and that's not very pleasant for adults. Comparison rarely makes one feel happy unless they're at the superior end of such comparison.

I have gotten away with many things under the grab of my youth. I like to think I'm mature for my age, but given the fact that most of my dealings are with people twice or thrice my age…being youthful (and yet prudent) gives me an advantage. Youth can often be forgiven (or even fondly praised) for their success by the older generations instead of being envied as a peer.

For example, the other day, I was on the cover of an international business magazine, and my parents' business acquaintances were pretty enthusiastic about it. Even threw me a party. I didn't really want to go, but Mum said it would be rude to turn it down. So Mum, Dad and I went. Big Brother was in Geneva doing some cool research thing that none of us understood, and Little Sister was off snorkelling in Grenada (it was her newest hobby).

We were welcomed with cheers and applause.

"What a splendid child you have," an elderly gentleman told my Dad, not bothering to lower his voice. "I can only wish my own son was half as good. I am a little envious, you know."

SEC comparisons are rather awkward when done in public. However, before Dad could respond, another lady spoke up.

"That's so true," she said wistfully. "I keep telling my children to be more like Seccy – but who listens to their parents these days…"

"I bet Seccy listens to his parents – that must be why he's so successful!" someone else piped up.

After an endless hour of similar exclamations, I sent my Mum a pleading look. Prior experience dictated that dating/marriage offers would start pouring in soon. I really wanted to escape before that.

Mum signalled Dad and the two of them worked seamlessly to present a perfectly plausible excuse that would get us out within minutes.

Exactly fifteen minutes later, we were in our car, heading home.

Mum ruffled my hair. "So, Seccy – how does it feel to be a celebrity?" she teased, her eyes sparkling with mirth.

"Tedious," I told her honestly. "The older people seemed overtly fond of me and the younger ones looked ready to murder me out of frustration."

Dad chuckled. "That's not an inaccurate description," he said. "Good thing we escaped when we did. I really didn't want to tackle the whole when-are-your-boys-getting-married thing. People have cooled down a little about your Big Brother…but you, Seccy, seem to be the hot favourite for a son-in-law these days."

I groaned piteously.

"Do you have someone you like?" Mum asked. "I'd like to hear about your youthful romance."

I pretended to be sound asleep for the rest of the journey.

27 ZENITH

Zenith (*noun*):
The highest peak of power or success or achievement.
Example: At the zenith of his career, he was unbeatable.

***

One of my closest friends once told me, "You know, Seccy, you're the person I'd least want to offend in my life."

"Why?" I asked, curious.

"Because you're dangerous," he replied.

I frowned at him, confused.

He laughed lightly. "Look – in your family, your Big Brother is the brainy one, your Little Sister is the talented one…and you – you are the dangerous one."

"But why?" I asked. I didn't think I was dangerous. If anything, I was the nicest and the most normal sibling. I was the SEC, wasn't I? I was the reachable goal, the imperfect one, the human one…not the demi-gods that my siblings were.

My friend looked rather frustrated, as if struggling to explain a simple concept to a particularly dense person.

I didn't like that look at all. I was a quick learner, and I prided myself on it.

My friend took a deep breath and said, "All right. Look at it this way. You are in your early twenties. You own a Fortune 500 company which you built from scratch. You wine and dine with bigshots twice or even thrice your age, and they actually listen to you when you talk business. More often than not, you can simply pick up the phone and sort out an issue that would take people months or years to tackle. And most importantly, you got yourself here step by step, working your way through all of it."

I felt rather flattered. "Well, I did get lucky to be adopted into this family," I told him.

He shook his head. "That's only a part of it. Being a child of a rich family – adopted or not – means an easy life for most people. You're naturally smart, you could have laid back and enjoyed life instead. You didn't need to work so hard to achieve things on your own. You didn't need to become as powerful as you are on your own; you could have simply relied on your parents. You'd still have been above average."

I honestly didn't understand his point. Why would I waste my life doing nothing?

My friend chuckled and shook his head fondly. "The fact that you don't even comprehend what I'm talking about…that's both adorable and scary. This is why you're the paragon of virtues my parents used to hold up as an example all the time. Not just my parents, pretty much everyone around. You…you're like the zenith of achievability."

Well, that was something I knew. And secretly enjoyed. But I still didn't understand how that made me dangerous. I prided myself on being a gentleman. And I never harmed anyone unless they tried to hurt my family. And even when I did, it was never anything as uncouth as a fistfight or a bloodbath (I'm squeamish anyway.) – I always resolved things cleanly and courteously and legally.

My friend shook his head again and patted my shoulder. "Just go home, Seccy," he said tiredly. "And ask your family."

Very well, then, I thought to myself, and did exactly that.

***

Mum, Dad, Big Brother and Little Sister burst out laughing when I told them.

I was flabbergasted.

Finally, Little Sister took pity on me. "Brother Seccy, look at it this way. Who is the most powerful among us in terms of money and influence?"

"Dad for money and Mum for influence," I said promptly. Dad was among the top ten richest people in the country, and Mum won some award or the other more often than she cared to remember; she had people begging her for interviews at least half a dozen times a day.

Dad shook his head, his eyes sparkling with mirth. "Don't you manage over 80% of my business these days?" he pointed out.

"Well, yes," I replied. "But…"

"And who do people call to make top-level decisions?" Mum continued. "Who represents us when there's something in the media?"

"Me, but…"

Mum flicked my forehead. "Silly child," she said. "Stop doubting yourself."

"I'm not!" I protested. Hello? I didn't lack confidence, all right?

"Seccy," Big Brother said. "You're the best of us all."

My jaw hit the floor. What the hell?

"How's that even possible?!" I demanded. "Big Brother, your research…"

"It's important, but I can indulge myself in it because I know you've got my back and are protecting everything I care about," he declared, not letting me finish.

"Yup," Little Sister said. "Same here. I do what I do because I know you're there to clean up the mess and to retaliate if someone tries to harm one of us." She winked cheekily. "Our knight in shining armour – Brother Seccy!"

I flushed. "Stop making fun of me."

"We're not," Mum said. "It's true."

"And we're very proud of you," Dad said.

"Yup," Little Sister agreed.

"Absolutely," Big Brother pitched in.

I was pleased and embarrassed in equal measures. It's not like I haven't received enough praise from the family growing up, but it's always good to hear your loved ones say that they're proud of you, isn't it? It's like a warm mug of chocolate (with maybe a little bit of rum in it) that flows smoothly down your throat and makes you feel cocooned and comfortable and safe.

Big Brother slung an arm around my shoulders. "Seccy, why don't you write a book? You've always wanted to, right?"

I shook my head. I had too much work.

"I'll help out with the company work," Little Sister offered. "Mum and Dad, too. Take some time off, relax and write. You've worked hard, Brother Seccy."

Mum pinched my cheeks. "That's true," she said. "You've even lost weight – look at you now. People will say Mum doesn't feed her second son."

Oh, please. Mum knew exactly how hard I had to work to prevent myself from putting on weight. Unlike Big Brother's lanky frame and Little Sister with her super active lifestyle, I had the unfortunate tendency to put on weight easily.

Dad chuckled. "It's a good idea. I think we should all take some time off and go somewhere. Seccy can stay on and write – or just laze off, let the poor boy decide that. The rest of us will come back and hold the fort while he's resting."

"I don't even know what to write about," I muttered.

"Write about yourself," Mum said, smiling. "All famous people write about themselves."

"I'm not famous," I retorted.

"Then write something that'll make you famous," Mum said.

I groaned. Hmm…perhaps I could write about business management? After all, that was my forte. Or…

"Don't write a book on management or business," Little Sister warned, halting that train of thought. "You'd better write a story."

"Yes, Your Highness," I grumbled.

She swatted at my head.

"No violence," Big Brother said, pulling me away to safety.

Mum and Dad burst out laughing.

This…this was the zenith of happiness, I thought. I don't know if the three of us will find well-matched spouses/partners in the future (notwithstanding Little Sister's secret paramour that only Big Brother knows about) and have a loving relationship like Mum and Dad – but that's something for later. For now, we're an odd but very happy family. We're enviable.

Which reminded me that Mum and Dad had never compared any of us to other kids or used a SEC example to make us do anything. It's fine for Big Brother and Little Sister, because they're so unique – but what about me? Didn't they compare me to anyone, ever? So I asked.

They laughed heartily. Big Brother and Little Sister looked at me as if I'd suddenly turned into an idiot.

Finally, Mum said, "Why on earth would we hold up someone else as an example for you to look at? You're fine the way you are."

"Besides," Dad added. "Other people use *you* as an example. Oh, boy, the envious looks I've gotten for having such excellent children!"

"Hear that, Brother Seccy? You're *exemplary*," Little Sister teased.

"That's a good thing," Big Brother said quickly, comforting me innocently.

Oh,   man.   I   was   a   lucky   guy.

ABOUT THE AUTHOR

Jayantika Ganguly, better known as Jay, is a corporate lawyer, a Sherlockian and a certified life coach, who likes to think of herself as a writer and a traveller. She has written a fair number of Sherlockian pastiches and essays in various international anthologies. This is her third standalone book.